ONE HUNDRED INTENTIONS

26

AN ASPEN COVE SMALL TOWN ROMANCE

KELLY COLLINS

BOOK NOOK PRESS

Cover design by Victoria Cooper Art *

Edits by Melissa Martin, Donna Wolz, Riet Strijker, Sabrina Medina

All trademarks are the property of their respective owners.

CHAPTER ONE

Reese Arden had a voice not even a mother could love. It wasn't a Fran Drescher ear-splitting sound, but more like an annoying skipping record kind of thing that had everyone filling in the blanks or running for earplugs.

"Mom, I'm f-f-f—"

"I know, you're fine. You're always fine."

Because words didn't flow easily from Reese's lips, people tended to speak for her. Her mother could have an entire conversation without Reese ever saying a word.

"I need this. I need a p-p-p—"

"A place to find inspiration. I know. Turn around and come home. Why can't you find it here? It's never been a problem in the thirty-two years we've lived together."

"M-m-m—"

"Don't mom me. I know you. What you need is a safe place."

"Mom," she said more forcefully. It wasn't her usual demeanor, but desperate times called for desperate measures. "I've l-l—"

"So, you've said. You've lost your muse. You won't find it in Aspen Cove. There's nothing for you there."

She let out a sigh that felt a mile long. It didn't pay to argue with the original helicopter parent. Some would call Reese a failure-to-launch kid. At thirty-two, she wasn't a kid, but she still lived at home. The first time she moved out wasn't a complete failure. She lived in the dorms at college and fared reasonably well until Charles. After graduating with her MFA, she worked at her mother's clinic and made minimum wage while trying to find her way in the publishing world. That was until she got a job ghostwriting. Once her mother figured out she might make it on her own with two jobs, she fired her. It turned out that her mother needed her far more than she cared to admit. Something told Reese that it was her mother who had failed to launch.

"You need to get a life, Mom, and I can't be the center."

Her mother gasped. "How can you say that? I've got a life, a job, and a home. Which is more than I can say for you."

And they were back to the crux of the problem. Reese was stuck where she started … at the mercy of her mother.

"Exactly, g-g-glad we're on the same page." She was about to be abrupt, so she tried to smooth things over. "Mom, you know I love you, but I've got to go."

She knew if she didn't cut the conversation short, her mother would convince her to turn around and go home. She always did, but Reese had a lot riding on this trip. Her creative muse, like Elvis, had left the building and hadn't been seen in months. She had a deadline to make and no time to play this game with her mother, so she turned off her phone and continued on the journey toward Aspen Cove.

Though she lived mostly in silence, her head was filled with loud thoughts. Those she couldn't quiet made it to the pages of a book. She was a New York Times Bestselling Author two times over, but as a ghostwriter, no one knew her name.

With the radio turned up and tuned into her favorite oldies station, she belted out a song about love. Too bad people didn't sing their way through life. If that were the case, she'd be an excellent verbal communicator. When she sang, her voice was fluid and flawless.

As she drove toward Aspen Cove, there were three things she knew for sure:

First, no one was interested in listening to her words unless they were put to paper.

Second, she needed more than her dog, Z, could give her. His sloppy kisses were nice, but they didn't fill the hollow in her heart. Sadly, love was a luxury she wasn't afforded. Outside of her mother's love, she'd experienced very little. A boyfriend in high school who shut her up with kisses each time she tried to speak, and a college guy who broke her heart. That deep connection she saw when she looked at couples in love had always evaded her.

Third, she needed her muse to return. Without her, no words hit the paper, and no words meant no money. No money meant no future. Without money, she'd be living with her mother until they both needed walkers.

Reese had ninety days to write a book. Ninety days because that was all Uncle Frank could offer. He was turning the lakefront property into an Airbnb because no one ever used it. Her mother hated the town and hadn't visited in ages. Uncle Frank was married to his job. Yep, love had eluded her entire family.

She thought about her need for love and laughed. "Maybe I can f-f-f-find a d-d-deaf man who would l-l-love me."

Z hopped from the back seat and sat in the passenger seat beside her with his head cocked to the side. Like most people who heard her speak, he always had that confused look about him, as if he were trying to decipher what she said. Once he realized the word "treat" wasn't part of her sentence, he curled into a ball and sighed.

"I know, b-b-big disappointment." That's what she'd always felt like. She wasn't the kid her mom expected, but the one she got. Hell as a teen parent, she was pretty sure Sara Arden would have passed on the whole pregnancy thing to begin with. Then there was the speech impediment. She didn't know why she stuttered. There'd been no childhood trauma she could recollect, no medical condition like a stroke or brain injury. All they could say was it was emotionally triggered.

A ball of anxiety got lodged in her throat each time she talked, and she choked on the words.

She glanced at Z, who looked like she'd tossed his favorite ball into the trashcan.

"You're g-g-going to l-l-love it in Aspen Cove." She wasn't sure if that was the truth, but she figured it would be more exciting than her mom's house in Oklahoma. "We're staying at the lake house. There's w-w-water and b-b-birds to chase." She'd spent some time there as a kid, but it had been decades since she'd been back. She had no actual memories of the place.

"It's cool Uncle Frank said I could stay," she said to Z. "He thinks I'm bringing some friends." She lifted her shoulders in a shrug. "It's not a lie. I'm bringing you." She ruffled his neck fur and smiled. "I told him that so he'd s-s-stay in S-S-Silver Springs. I love the man, but I can't stand the p-p-pitiful looks he gives me."

At that thought, she wondered if she should have been honest with him. Sometimes she wondered if she was her own worst enemy.

Z covered his muzzle with his paw, but she still saw the beautiful blue of his eyes. With her mother being a veterinarian, there were always animals around the house. Z was fierce looking when he wanted to be, but he was all marshmallow and cream inside.

She cranked up the music and listened to Otis Redding singing about tenderness.

"I was born in the wrong era, Z." She was always drawn to the music of the fifties and sixties. The blues and Motown were her favorites. She could turn on the music and dance for hours by herself, probably because no one was standing in line to dance with her.

As she wound along the mountain road, she kept the music playing. In the distance, she saw a man standing on the soft shoulder with his thumb out. From what she could see, he was dressed in camouflage pants and carried a rucksack.

There was no way, no how, she'd pick up a hitchhiker. She'd done some silly things in her life like mix wine and liquor—yep, never been sicker—but she wasn't stupid. A woman traveling alone didn't pick up drifters.

Just as she approached, the volume rose as "Stop in the Name of Love" screamed at her. Startled, she slammed on the brakes. Her car fishtailed and slid across the gravel before coming to a stop beside the hitchhiking soldier.

"What the hell?" Her hand came to rest over her pounding heart. She nearly ran over the guy.

The Supremes continued to sing, but all she heard was her mother's voice, loud and clear, telling her to be more careful.

The man walked forward, and Z popped up to look out the window. He was wary of strangers. It was probably a learned behavior he got from her. Whenever she took him for a walk, she avoided people, even crossing the street to ensure no interaction.

The voice in her head shouted louder than her mother's warning about stranger danger. It said, *Open the window, open your life.* She knew it was her subconscious again, pushing her internal envelope.

Her natural instinct was to put on the gas and take off, but she'd nearly run the man over and felt obligated to make sure he was okay.

She took a good look at him to make sure he didn't seem like a serial killer. She had no idea if there was a profile for people who murdered at will, but he looked harmless enough. She took the rest of him in. His brown hair and brown eyes didn't look dangerous ... they looked sad despite the forced smile on his face.

The name tag sewn into the pocket of his jacket read Fearless. Was that a sign? One that said she should fear less? Of course not. It was his name, not a set of life's rules for her.

Inside his pocket was a pink envelope peeking out. Her writer's brain went to work making up his story without him saying a word. Was it a Dear John letter from a lost love? A map leading him on a journey? Or simply a bill collector who had good taste in envelopes?

He looked at her with confusion, and rightly so. She'd stopped and hadn't even spoken a word. Her car idled next to him with her window closed. Maybe he thought she was a serial killer.

Before she chickened out and hightailed it up the road, she cracked the window a little and smiled. Sometimes a smile spoke the words she couldn't.

"Thanks for stopping." Despite the volume of the music, the deep timbre of his voice danced across her skin, leaving goosebumps in its wake.

Z stuck his nose to the crack and tried to lick the man. That was odd behavior for him, but maybe he was lonely too and needed more than her. Maybe he craved male attention as much as she did.

She nodded and kept smiling, certain she looked like a crazy person. Diana Ross and the Supremes ended their demands, and she reached over to turn down the volume.

He didn't seem to notice she hadn't said a thing.

"Hey, boy," the man said, sliding a couple of fingers inside the window to stroke Z's soft ear. "I'm heading to Aspen Cove." He stood and nodded toward the north. "I'd appreciate a ride if you're up for some company."

The thought of company and having to talk to this man made her skin break out in a cold sweat, but she had nearly run him down, so she reluctantly nodded and unlocked the door.

Pointing to the back seat, she said, "Z." He was an intuitive dog. And because she spoke little, he learned to follow her hand and head signals. Too bad people weren't as perceptive.

The man pointed to his duffel bag. "Back seat or trunk?"

She popped the trunk and waited for him to situate his belongings and take his place in the passenger side. When he did, he smiled warmly and said, "I'm Brandon. Thanks for the lift."

She put the car into drive and pulled back onto the highway without a word.

She wondered how long she could remain silent and decided she at least owed him a name. "R-Reese," she said quietly, hoping he didn't notice the stutter.

The first word was out, and it wasn't too painful. A minor blip, but all in all, it was okay.

"Where are you headed?" he asked.

She took a deep breath and willed herself to articulate. The last thing she wanted to see was that deer in the headlights look. It was the look men got just before they bolted from her presence. She wanted to laugh because she'd sped up to forty miles per hour. Any exit at this point would be painful for him.

"Aspen Cove," she said without a blip.

He nodded. "Same as me. Cool. As I said, I appreciate the ride." He adjusted his seat, so his knees weren't touching the dash. "I don't want to seem ungrateful, but would you mind if I took a little siesta? I've been thumbing it since I left Texas several days ago, and I'm beat."

She shook her head, not minding one bit.

He leaned his seat farther back, far enough for Z to lay his head on the headrest. "Crank up the music if you want. I've slept through worse."

She wasn't sure if he meant the noise or her taste in tunes. The oldies were still playing in the background with Dinah Shore's "What a Diff'rence a Day Makes." It was her Grandma Mae's favorite song.

She turned it up and listened to words about hope and the end of loneliness. Somehow, it all seemed fitting. It was as if the universe had created a playlist just for her today.

Although she wasn't talking to Brandon, she had spoken to him and survived. Some might say she was still alone, but a glance at the man who was already asleep proved she wasn't. Just his presence made her feel less lonely.

She drove through the winding mountain pass and admired the scenery. Nature had it right. There were tall pines nestled next to sparsely leafed aspens. From the crack of a giant gray boulder grew a tiny purple flower.

Differences shouldn't set people apart but give them a reason to come together. One's weakness could quickly become another one's strength. The tall pines protected the tiny aspens, and the fragile flower gave beauty to the rigid stone. Too bad she couldn't find someone who could be the yin to her yang. The sun to her moon. The voice to her silence.

The last fifty minutes of her trip were spent in reflection and making side glances at the handsome stranger who hitchhiked to Aspen Cove from Texas. She wanted to know his story—wanted to know what that pink envelope he protectively placed his hand over meant to him.

As she entered the tiny town, she pulled in front of The Corner Store and parked. It was the first stop on her journey and the last for theirs together. Why did she feel so sad to say goodbye to someone she hadn't truly met? They exchanged names, and that was it, but somehow, it seemed like more.

She reached over and tapped his shoulder, and he nearly flew out of his seat. She jumped back and hit her head on the window.

"Shit ..." He shook his head. "I mean, shoot. I'm sorry."

She rubbed at the spot on her head and smiled, hoping to convey that she was okay even though it was already swelling into a nice little egg.

He seemed to understand that she was signaling she was fine, but still, he frowned.

"That's what we all say, but are we ever truly fine?"

CHAPTER TWO

"Is here, okay?" she asked.

He looked around to see where they were. "Is this Aspen Cove?"

She squinted her eyes as if the pain was severe but dropped her hand from the back of her head, nodded, and smiled.

He wasn't sure if she would say anything, but her lips opened and closed as if she was considering it.

"Y-y-yes," she said and let her head drop.

He wondered if he made her nervous. He had that effect on many people. He was big and burly and had been told occasionally that if he wasn't smiling, he looked like he was prepping for murder.

He forced the corners of his lips up to soften his naturally stern look.

"I appreciate the ride," he said.

He took her in, from her curly reddish hair to her green eyes and that lovely smile—a smile that reminded him of his sister, Gwen.

If not for her, and a million unanswered questions, he wouldn't be here. He placed his hand over his jacket pocket to ensure the letter was still there. That was the true reason he was in the tiny Colorado mountain town.

He'd read the letter a thousand times. It was from a woman named Bea Bennett, and it spoke of her daughter Brandy, who had passed in a car accident.

Understanding his sister's death had been like decoding a top-secret message. From what he could gather, his sister had been the recipient of Brandy's donor liver ten years ago. That's about all he knew at this point.

He opened the door. "Thanks for the ride." He climbed out and turned his face to the sky, letting the warmth of the sun soak in.

Coming from the open door was the song "The Letter." He only knew it because his sister loved the oldies and sang that song all the time. What were the odds?

He bent over and looked inside the car. "Can you pop the trunk?"

She blushed and nodded, pressing the release button, and the trunk popped open.

The dog hopped up and tried to exit, but Brandon stopped him.

"You stay here, buddy." He rubbed the Malamute's ear and listened to him groan, then turned to Reese. "Take care, okay?"

She rolled down the windows a little and killed the engine.

"You, too. Hope you find whatever you came here for."

He nodded and smiled. So, she didn't stutter. Maybe he'd imagined it.

"Why are you here?" he asked. Aspen Cove didn't seem like a destination location. It was a pass-through town on the way to something better.

She stared at him but didn't answer.

He stepped back. "Well, I hope you find what you're looking for, too." He shut the door and walked behind the car to get his bag from the trunk. Once on the sidewalk, he glanced around the town. It was a single block long; with not much more than The Corner Store he was standing in front of.

His stomach grumbled. His options were an unappealing frozen burrito and a bag of chips from the little store or the diner down the street. He'd eaten most of his meals from little holes in the walls along the way, so he moved down the sidewalk to a place called Maisey's. The door opened in front of him and two men in uniform walked out, carrying the smell of bacon with them. The rumbling in his stomach grew louder, so he hoisted his bag to his back and opened the diner door. The bell above jingled loudly as he walked inside.

"Take a seat anywhere, sweetheart. I'll be right with ya," a blonde waitress called from the register. She was ringing up an older man who looked straight out of a Wilford Brimley commercial with his bushy mustache and brows to match.

The older man paid his bill. "Thank you for your service, son," he said as he shuffled past Brandon

"My pleasure to serve, sir." It was the truth ... sort of. He would have rather been a race car driver or an astronaut, but those jobs didn't go to kids raised in the foster care system who graduated from high school with a GED. He'd joined the service for one reason. Gwen needed rehab, and he needed money to pay for it. It was that simple.

He moved toward the lit-up jukebox and took the booth beside it. In front of him sat an upside-down coffee mug and a metal rack that held menus. He shimmied one free and saw the usual diner fare like an all-day breakfast and a blue-plate special. In his experience, you could never go wrong with the daily special.

Swinging a coffee pot between two fingers, the waitress approached.

"Cup of joe?"

He nodded and turned the mug over so she could fill it up.

"You're new in town. Just passin' through or stayin' a bit?" Her eyes went to the envelope in his pocket. "That right there tells me you'll be around a while."

He pulled out the tattered envelope and set it on the table. "You know something about this?"

She shook her head. "Nope, that one there is as unique as the woman who sent it. But I've seen a few like it."

He poked the envelope, shifting it in a circle. "You know where I can find this Bea Bennett?"

Her eyes widened. "Sure." The woman whose tag read Maisey filled his cup. "She lives up on the hill above town now." She finished pouring, set down the pot, and took an order pad from her pocket. "You want anything else, or will coffee do it for you?"

"I'll take the blue-plate special."

She wrote it down, then looked him in the eye. "You want to know what it is?"

He didn't care. "Nope, it's got to be better than a bean burrito or a field ration."

"You ain't setting the bar too high."

He chuckled. "I've learned not to expect too much."

"You're too young to be that cynical. Wait until you get your first wrinkle." She picked up the pot, pivoted, and walked toward the kitchen.

Maisey was blind as a bat if she didn't see how unkind the years had been to him. His eyes were etched with lines of worry and self-hatred. His body was scarred by wars he'd fought in the world, but no one saw the ones marring his soul. Those were wounds that continued to weep and would until the day he died.

At thirty-four, he was cynical, but he had every reason to be. He'd been abandoned by his parents, who thought getting high was more important than raising two kids. When the system separated him and his sister, he felt deserted once more. It became clear that

Gwen was what you would call "the good one." But he learned quickly, it wasn't as if she wasn't as wild or delinquent as him, she was just better at hiding it.

The truth was, he acted out his disappointments in anger while she simmered in silence.

Maisey breezed by in a cloud of perfume, leaving him a plate of fried chicken, mashed potatoes, and green beans.

"If this ain't the best meal you've had all week, it's on the house."

"Oh, I'll be paying. My last meal was a bag of gummy worms."

"You got a sweet tooth? If so, you'll want to finish this off with pie. Apple or cherry?" She stepped back and eyed him. "Oh hell, I'll bring you both. You're a big boy."

"Much obliged, ma'am."

Her cheeks turned pink. "I haven't been called ma'am in years. Most women would cuff your ear for that, but I like it. It makes me feel all proper and all. You from the south?"

He was from all over, but he was born in Dallas and spent most of his early days there.

"I'm a Texan through and through," he said. The funny thing about being born in Texas was it was more like a religion or a nationality than a place. Texas ran through the veins like blood. Everything was bigger in Texas, from hair, to smiles, to heartache.

"You enjoy, and like Doc said, thank you for your service."

"You're welcome." What was he supposed to say to that? He served honorably. He was a patriot. What started as a paycheck—a means to an end—became a part of who he was. The Army taught him many things. Most of all, it taught him how to be responsible. At least until Gwen died. It was then that he realized, like his parents, he'd abandoned the only thing he'd truly loved ... her. He'd joined up to pay for rehab and to save her but lost her, anyway.

He let go of the sorrow filling his heart and filled his empty spaces with fried chicken and mashed potatoes. He was doing more than filling up his belly. He was shoring up his reserves, so he had the energy to get through the day.

He hoped to get answers. Bea Bennett had to know more than he did. She knew his sister needed a liver, which was more information than he had known. Why hadn't Gwen told him she had hepatitis? He found that out by a slip of paper tucked inside a shoebox. A diagnosis from the rehab center he paid for. Why didn't she call when her liver was failing, or when a donor's liver was found? Why did the doctors give an opioid addict an opioid for pain? Did they know? Had she kept that from them in the same way she kept everything else from him? Her simmering silence held secrets and felt like a complete betrayal.

CHAPTER THREE

Reese looked over her shoulder at Z, whose nose was pressed to the glass. It broke her heart that she had to leave him in the car, but she didn't know the rules in town. Lots of places were pet-friendly these days, but many were not.

She walked into the cute little store and picked up a basket. Uncle Frank told her there were essentials like spices and condiments in the house, but other than that, the refrigerator was empty.

"Welcome," the woman sitting behind the counter said. Her smile was warm and her demeanor friendly.

"Hi," Reese answered.

"Can I help you find something?"

She shook her head.

The woman slid from her stool and walked from behind the counter. Waddle was more like it. She was very pregnant and shifted from side to side to propel herself forward. Her hands laid on the top of her belly like it was a table, and in truth, it resembled one.

"Wow, you're..." She didn't know how to finish that sentence because any word she blurted would seem insensitive.

"Big as a house?"

Reese felt awful for saying anything. Because she was often as silent as a mouse, she didn't know what compelled her to say anything at all.

"Glowing."

The woman laughed. "That's probably because the little urchin is cutting off my blood supply." She tapped her rounded belly. "I swear nothing is circulating below my rib cage." She bent over and looked at the edge of the shiny stainless steel display rack. "Are my cheeks red?"

What was Reese supposed to say? She didn't know the woman and wasn't sure if winter-kissed cheeks in the summer were the norm for this girl. They were in the mountains and closer to the sun. Despite it being June, the air in the Rockies was often crisp and cool.

"You l-look healthy." She smiled, feeling confident that what she said wouldn't offend. "W-w-w-when are you d-d-due?" She gripped the basket so hard trying to get the words out that she was certain she'd embedded the metal handle into her palm.

"Yesterday." She rubbed her tummy. "There are three of us due the same week, and we are all late. Must be the mountain air." She wiped her hands on the hem of her shirt. "By the way, I'm Beth."

"You're still w-working?"

She laughed. "Now you sound like my husband." She raised her hands in the air. "There's only so much nesting you can do. Besides, I like meeting people and talking to them. Pretty soon all I'll have is my meddling mom, my always-worried husband, and a baby to talk to. I'm socializing while I can. Are you just passing through?"

Reese shook her head. She couldn't say she was passing through since her family had roots there. "I'm Reese Arden."

"Arden." Beth looked up at the decorative tin ceiling as if the answers were hammered into the design. "Oh, Frank's ..." She tilted her head to the side.

"Niece."

"Well, Frank's niece. What can I help you find?" She took a step forward, winced, and grabbed her stomach, stumbling backward until she could grip the counter. "Wow, that was a big one."

Reese felt the blood drain from her face. "L-labor?" She wasn't good in a crisis and didn't know what to do if Beth went into labor. She wasn't familiar with the town and didn't even know if there was a doctor nearby. "Not now." She hated how she resorted to monosyllabic words. They were often easy for her, but her spoken vocabulary didn't do her justice.

Beth sucked in a breath and stood straight. "Nope, Grayson has a mean kick. I swear he's leading a troupe of Irish river dancers inside me."

Reese nodded toward the stool. "Sit."

"You're probably right." She swiped a package of Little Debbie Nutty Bars from the end cap. "It's snack time, anyway." She turned it over and looked at the ingredient list. "It's got peanut butter. That's healthy, right?"

"Sure."

Reese loosened her grip on the basket and walked down the aisles. The shop was charming, with open wooden baskets of overflowing produce and roughhewn shelves neatly lined with canned goods. The outside walls had rows of refrigeration units etched with dairy, meat, and frozen goods in the glass.

She gathered everything she needed to get by for a few days and headed to the register to check out.

In front of Beth were two more Little Debbie wrappers.

"That good, huh?" She'd never had a Nutty Bar or a Cosmic Brownie, but she'd seen them on the shelf.

"I put on ten pounds from Swiss Rolls alone." She patted her tummy. "Thirty-five pounds and probably only seven of it is a baby." She rang up Reese's groceries and gave her the total.

Reese had limited funds until the book she was supposed to work on was complete, but *Love's Lost Flame* hadn't sparked her interest from the beginning. The characters were straight out of a pirate parody.

She reached into her bag for cash. "You're good." She was referring to the woman's weight. Though she knew little about pregnancy and what she was supposed to gain, the woman looked healthy, and she had a glow about her. A tiny spark of envy burned in Reese's belly. She was already passing her window of opportunity for children. With no man in sight, she imagined she'd be relegated to Z and, when he passed, a houseful of cats or hamsters.

Beth laughed. "I won't be good if I don't lay off the snacks." She bagged the groceries. "You have kids?"

At the mention, Reese's womb twisted and ached. She'd always wanted kids, but you had to have a love interest or a sperm donor to get one, and she had neither.

"I've got a boy named Z."

Beth's eyes widened. "How old is he?"

Reese laughed. "Thirty-five." He was five, but she always thought of his age in dog years versus human years. He'd just recently passed her up.

Beth gave her a strange look.

"Malamute," Reese clarified.

"Oh ... a dog."

"My fur baby." She looked toward the door. "Car."

"Next time, bring him in. Jewel, the store owner, won't mind. Hell, I'm pretty sure you can bring him anywhere you want in town. We're a family-friendly town and that includes pets. Sage, who owns the bed and breakfast, has a three-legged dog named Otis. Her husband has a one-eyed cat named Mike."

"Match made in heaven." Beth was easy to talk to and didn't create that lump in her throat. It wasn't often she found someone who put her at ease. Then again, she spent most of her time with her mom and that woman made her want to cut her tongue out.

"Katie has a Labrador named Bishop, and Sage's sister Lydia and her husband Wes have Sarge, a German Shepherd. Deanna has a poodle, but I can't remember his name."

Reese smiled and nodded, not wanting to push her luck and get stuck in an endless loop on a word.

Beth inhaled sharply and let out her breath slowly. "That one was different."

"You, okay?"

Beth panted. "Umm, I don't think so." She stepped from behind the counter and looked down at the puddle at her feet. "Can you get Doc Parker?"

"Who?"

Beth gripped the counter and groaned. "Uh, oh."

Panic rose inside Reese. "W-w-w-what do you mean, uh, oh?"

Beth gripped the hem of her skirt and pulled it up. "He's coming ... now."

Reese dropped her groceries and counted to three as Beth groaned.

"Get. Doc. Now," she cried.

"Get d-d-d-doc, n-n-now. Right." Who the hell was Doc?

Reese ran from the store like her tail was on fire. She stopped on the sidewalk and skimmed the storefronts. There was a diner and a hairdresser, a bakery, and a tackle shop. There was even a pharmacy right next door, but nothing shouted medical facility until she saw the red flashing light ... Doctor is in.

"Thank goodness." She bolted through the pharmacy door and came upon an older woman sitting behind the counter. "I n-n-need a d-d-doctor."

The woman with blue-gray hair looked up from her crossword puzzle. "You look fine."

"N-n-no. The b-b-b-b-baby is coming."

The woman cocked her head. "You're pregnant? You're as big as a minute."

Reese stomped her foot. "Where's the doctor?" She sounded like she was ready to spit fire.

A voice came from above. "What's all that racket down there? Lovey ... are you okay?"

"Someone's having a baby."

"I'll be right down." There was a *clip-clop shuffle* on the stairs, and an old, white-haired man appeared carrying a black bag. "Who's up?" He looked at Reese. "Do I know you?"

"No." She pointed toward the far wall. "Your patient is next door." If he took as long to get next door as he did to get down the stairs, that kid could celebrate his first birthday before they got there.

"Then, let's go." He stopped halfway and went back to kiss the woman behind the counter. "I'll meet you at the diner for dinner, Lovey."

"Hurry!"

The old codger grumbled something under his breath about youth and disrespect as he shuffled forward.

"Lead the way."

When they entered the store, Beth was on the floor in a pool of water. She was on the phone crying until her next pain came and she screamed, "Dammit, Gray, get here now. I can see your son's head."

Doc picked up his pace and dropped to his knees before Beth. "You did half the work without me."

He looked at Reese. "Go upstairs and grab a pillow and a blanket. We aren't going anywhere."

"I don't want to have my baby on the floor of The Corner Store," Beth yelled.

"You don't get to choose."

Another contraction hit her, and Beth screamed, sending Reese running upstairs into someone's residence to pilfer a pillow and a blanket from the bed.

When she came back, Doc tucked the pillow under Beth's head, then turned to Reese.

"You ever deliver a baby?"

"W-w-what? N-n-no."

Doc tossed her a pair of gloves. "Glove up. Today is your day. Lydia and Sage are in Copper Creek, so you're my new nurse."

"I c-c-can't."

"Too late."

As he covered Beth's legs with a blanket, the door opened, and a big man rushed in. "Baby, I'm here."

"Welcome to the party, Gray. Are you ready to meet your son?" Doc looked at Beth. "Let's have a good push."

Everything happened so quickly that Reese wasn't sure if she was actually present or if she was in a nightmare. In one moment, the cashier was ringing up her groceries and eating a snack, and the next, Reese was holding a baby who looked like he'd been dipped in Crisco. A half an hour later, the mom and dad were cooing over their son. Once the ambulance arrived from Copper Creek, the little family was loaded up and only she and Doc remained.

Doc packed up his little black bag. "Mop's in the closet; lock up when you're done."

"Wait? What?"

CHAPTER FOUR

Brandon finished his chicken and mopped up the mashed potatoes and gravy with a biscuit that Maisey dropped off. The woman was like one of those bullet trains he'd heard about in Japan. They zipped by so fast, you wouldn't have known they'd even passed except your hair stood up from the wind they generated.

The door opened and in walked the old man again. Only this time, he had a big smile on his face. He threw his hands up in the air. "Well, one down and two to go."

Maisey let out a squeal that could be heard a mile away.

"Who was it?"

The man they called Doc shuffled to the corner booth and sank into the red bench.

He rubbed his bushy mustache and turned his coffee mug over, readying it for a fill-up. "Beth gave birth right there on the floor of The Corner Store."

Maisey gasped. "No."

"I'm telling you, the little critter was halfway out before I even got there. Had to enlist the help of some woman I don't even know. Have you seen her?"

Maisey glanced around the diner, her eyes stopping on Brandon. "Only stranger in town is that one over yonder."

Brandon smiled and nodded in their direction.

"Her name is Reese," he said.

Doc raised his hand to Maisey's height. "About this here tall and eyes like muddy moss?"

Brandon was certain if the woman who gave him a ride was here, she'd be offended. They weren't even his eyes, and he was offended for her.

"Pretty smile and eyes like emeralds? Yep, that's her." He wasn't much for words and his didn't do her justice, but at least he wouldn't leave with the muddy moss descriptor stuck in his head.

"You know her?"

Brandon shook his head. "Can't say I do, but she gave me a ride into town." He pulled a twenty-dollar bill from his pocket and held it in the air. "Can I settle my bill?"

Maisey poured Doc a cup of coffee and moved toward him. "But you didn't have any pie."

He patted his stomach. "There isn't room for pie."

Just before she got to him, she did a one-eighty and went straight for the pie case. "Nonsense, you're a growing boy and you need a piece of pie. Apple or cherry? If you don't choose, I'll give you both like I planned from the start."

If the worst thing that could happen was someone wanting to give him pie, he'd take it. He learned long ago to never leave too many variables open and never ask what's next because the universe had a way of obliging. People always said that God never gave you more than you could handle, but he disagreed. He'd been full up for some time now. Not wanting more than his stomach could take, he chose.

"Cherry please."

"That-a-boy," she said as she pulled a tin from the display case and scooped out a piece just for him. "You want whipped cream or ice cream?"

"Neither."

She rolled her eyes. "Okay then, both."

Before he could count to five, he had a piece of pie with a mountain of whipped topping and a scoop of ice cream the size of his fist.

"What brings you to town, son?" the older man asked from his place in the corner.

"I'm here to see Bea Bennett."

The man's bushy brows rose so high, Brandon was pretty confident they'd touch the man's hairline.

"She ain't very chatty lately."

Maisey rushed over to Doc's table. She stood in front of him so Brandon couldn't see the man or hear what the waitress said.

When Maisey moved, Doc was smiling. "But I'm sure she'll be pleased you came." His eyes went to where the pink envelope sat on the table. "I hope you find what you're looking for."

Brandon picked up the letter that seemed to get a lot of attention and tucked it back into his pocket.

The door opened, and the bell rang. In walked an older woman with silver-blue hair. She glanced around and made a beeline straight to the corner booth.

A few minutes later, the door opened again and in walked Reese, looking apprehensive. Her curls were pointing in every direction. Sidled up next to her was Z.

Maisey took in the woman and the dog. She frowned but quickly made the corners of her lips turn up.

"I'm assuming that's a support animal?" She nodded as she smiled.

Reese looked down at the Malamute. "No."

He knew exactly what Maisey was getting at.

"Yep, it's an emotional support dog," he said. "She doesn't go anywhere without him." Under his breath, he whispered. "She can only let him in if he's medically required."

"Oh," Reese said. "Yes." She moved farther into the diner and looked around at the tables and booths.

He pointed to the seat across from him. "Join me." He stabbed his pie with his fork.

She looked like she might dash out the door. He could see the indecision cross her features.

"I don't bite." He took a bite of ice cream and let it melt over his tongue. "Hard, that is."

His joke seemed to ease her somewhat, and she plopped onto the bench across from him and sighed. The dog inched his way under the table and curled up next to her feet.

Maisey rushed over. "Welcome to Aspen Cove. If you're Reese Arden, I have something for you."

Brandon chuckled. "If she gives you a choice between two things, choose one, or you'll get more than you bargained for." He pointed to his giant-sized serving.

"G-g-good to know." She turned to Maisey. "Coffee and w-w-whatever is good to eat." Her cheeks turned red like the cherry filling in his pie.

Maisey set the coffeepot down and fisted her hips. "Honey, everything I make is good." She nodded toward his empty plate. "What about the blue plate special? He seemed to like it." She glanced down at the dog. "Anything for the big guy there?"

Reese pointed to the plate and nodded and then pointed to the dog and shook her head.

Maisey emptied her pot of coffee, grounds, and all, into Reese's mug and left.

"Rumor has it you delivered a baby."

Her jaw dropped open, but she snapped it shut. "C-c-c-c-can you b-b-believe it?"

Her stutter seemed to get worse as she spoke. He could see it pained her, but he sat and waited.

"Is that what you do?"

She shook her head. "No."

That word was clear.

"How did you get roped into it?"

She shrugged and lifted her hands. "W-w-w-wrong p-p-p." She sighed and snapped her mouth closed.

He watched as frustration tightened her features, and a tear pooled in her eye. She swiped it away before it fell.

"S-s-sorry."

"Hey," he said sternly. "You don't need to be. I know what overwhelmed looks like and feels like." He touched his pocket and buttoned the envelope inside.

Maisey set the meal in front of her. "It's on the house. I hear you helped deliver Beth and Gray's baby today. Thank you for that."

Reese nodded.

Maisey pulled an envelope from her pocket. "Your uncle told me to give this to you when you arrived." She set it on the table.

It was a plain white envelope. There didn't seem to be anything special about it, but Reese picked it up and held it to her chest. It was obviously important to her.

He understood the importance of a single piece of correspondence. He was ending his tour in Afghanistan when he was notified of his sister's death. It came as a shock. He'd talked to her several weeks before and though she sounded tired, she said she was fine, but she was anything but fine.

If he went back a few years, he could see all the signs he missed, like the dullness of her eyes. She was always thin, but the last time he saw her, she looked undernourished. They fought about drug use because he thought she was using again. She marched him to a testing site where she came back negative. He went back to Afghanistan because he felt confident, she was telling the truth. The test didn't lie but Gwen did.

All he could figure at this point was that she was in liver failure again, and she said nothing.

"You okay?"

His brows must have furrowed. "Just thinking about life and how often we let it pass by with little thought."

She nodded and took a bite of a chicken leg.

"For years, I've been letting life rule me instead of the other way around. I didn't realize it until this moment."

She swallowed and pointed to his jacket. "Soldier."

It wasn't a question, but a statement of fact, and he wanted to know what that meant to her.

"Yeah, so?"

"You do ..." She swallowed several times before continuing. "What y-y-you ..." She groaned.

He could see how challenging it was for her. He didn't know her, but he thought her courageous. He could see that talking was not her favorite pastime. For Reese, it was an arduous task, and he bet it sapped her strength.

"You do what you're told," she blurted in one quick sentence.

That was true. He followed a set of rules and while he was a freethinker, there wasn't much opportunity to do it when he was part of a platoon with a mission. You followed the rules, or someone got hurt.

"Yep, you're right. They say jump and I ask how high."

She shook her head. "N-n-not what I meant."

He shrugged. "But it's true."

She peeled the skin off the chicken breast and took several chunks of white meat that she fed to Z.

"He's a good dog. How long have you had him?"

She raised her hand and splayed out five fingers.

"You're lucky."

She nodded.

He glanced out the window and saw the sky turning orange.

"I should get going. I've got a woman to meet."

He drew another bill from his pocket and added it to the twenty already on the table.

"Thanks for the ride, Reese." He smiled and told her what his sister always told him. "Be a good human." He wished she would have taken her own advice. Part of being a good human was caring for yourself because if you weren't at your best, you couldn't serve others.

He rose and approached Maisey.

"Where did you say I could find Bea?"

CHAPTER FIVE

The envelope sat in front of her like a welcome mat. As soon as she was finished with her meal, she opened it.

Dear Reese,

Welcome to Aspen Cove. You may not remember, but you spent a week one summer here as a kid. Here's the key to the house. I've loaded up the wine rack for you. Wasn't it Hemingway who said, "Write drunk and edit sober?" Hope you and your friends find your muses.

With love,

Uncle Frank

"How about some pie?"

Reese jumped in her seat at Maisey's voice. Her hand went to her heart, which beat so hard and quick, she could feel it through her shirt.

"No."

"Are you sure? It's the best in town." She chuckled. "It's the only pie in town unless you count those store-bought snacks down at The

Corner Store." Maisey moved toward the empty bench and plopped down across from her. "Does he have hair?"

Reese repeated the conversation in her head, trying to track it from pies to hair.

"The b-b—"

"Yes, the baby."

She sighed. It didn't matter where she was. Impatience ran rampant in the world, and no one had time to wait for her words.

"No."

Maisey smiled. "They are just as cute bald. I just love me some baby snuggles. We're in a population peak with more babies being born than people dying. For a while there we were in a slump. Now if my daughter-in-law and Deanna would get on it, we'd be done for now ... unless you're planning on blessing this town with a little one." She leaned in. "You know ... you and that soldier would make some beautiful babies together."

Reese shook her head. "We're not t-t-to—"

Maisey waved her hand through the air like she was swatting flies. "I know, but you could be."

The door opened as a middle-aged man and woman entered. The woman stepped inside and shouted, "I'm a grandma!"

She rushed over to Doc and shook his hand. There was some conversation, and then all eyes turned to Reese's booth. She was never comfortable being the center of attention. She always seemed to fail under others' expectations. It wasn't always that way. One year she was a sassy five-year-old who wanted to be an Olympic swimmer despite never swimming, and the next she was a bookworm.

"Looks like you're getting company." Maisey slid from the booth. "I'll bring you that pie." She grabbed the empty dishes and Brandon's money and left just in time for the woman and man to approach.

"Hello, I'm Elsa and this is my husband, Trenton. We understand you volunteered to help deliver Grayson, our grandson."

She wouldn't exactly call it volunteering because she wasn't given much choice, but at this point, it didn't matter. She'd helped bring a baby into this world. She could hardly believe it.

"Happy to help." The words came out clear, and she wondered why sometimes it was a chore and other times it was so easy.

"Are you new in town?"

She could try to explain that her family had property on the lake, but that might take hours for her to get the words out, so she nodded.

"We're new too. Well, we've been here for some months. The point is there is no stranger in town. There are two more babies due any moment, so be at the ready. Doc said you were a natural."

The man turned to Maisey, who was pouring Doc some coffee. "I'll pick up dinner tonight."

"You can get tomorrow. I already got tonight," Maisey said.

Trenton turned and smiled at her. "Looks like you'll be here for supper all week. The one thing I know for sure is that the people of Aspen Cove are generous, and there will be lots of thank you meals coming your way. Funeral meals come in casserole dishes, but birth meals are enjoyed at the diner."

The door flung open and a cute blonde rushed in. "I hear we have a baby."

Elsa joined the blonde, and they hopped up and down like schoolgirls who'd gotten their first kiss, giggling and squealing. "How much did he weigh?"

They both looked at Reese for an answer.

"The p-p-produce scale said seven pounds, six ounces."

Maisey returned with a piece of pie covered in whipped topping. Next to it was a scoop of ice cream the size of a grapefruit.

Once the women calmed down, the blonde approached. "I'm Katie Bishop and you're Reese Arden."

"How did you know?"

"Small town gossip travels at the speed of sound. Maisey is married to Ben, and Ben is my father-in-law, which makes Maisey my mother-in-law." She shook her head. "Ben called Bowie, who is my husband. He remembers you."

"Really?" Reese had no memories of Aspen Cove.

Katie took the seat across from her. "Yes, he said you played in the lake with them one summer until—"

The door opened, and an entire group entered. There was a man and a woman and at least a half dozen kids.

"Ben," Maisey yelled. "Drop more chicken. Lots more chicken."

Before she knew it, the diner was completely full of residents celebrating the newest addition to town. Eventually, everyone forgot she was there, and she pulled enough money from her bag to pay for her meal. Even though Maisey said it was on the house, she would never take advantage. She gathered Z and walked outside. The sun was setting, and the sky was a color orange that bled into purple.

She climbed into her car and drove down the main street to Lake Circle, where she took a left and pulled into the driveway next to B's Bed and Breakfast. That was one thing she remembered. The older woman who lived there gave her cookies, and she made the best lemonade known to man. Maybe that was the memory of a child, but in her recollection, she'd never had better.

"Are you ready?"

Z whined at the door and spun in circles in the seat. It was funny to watch such a big dog command such a small space.

"Let's go, boy. The f-f-future awaits." She patted her thigh and Z jumped over the center console and hopped from the car to the pine-needle-covered ground. He took in his surroundings, but then stared at her as if asking for permission to play.

"L-l-let's get unpacked and then you c-c-can play." The dog definitely understood every word she said. His shoulders slumped forward like a kid who'd been told it was time for bed.

She opened the trunk and tugged out her suitcase. She'd packed little because all she planned to do was write. All she needed was comfy clothes and fuzzy socks.

Dragging the suitcase up the driveway, she fished the key from her pocket. Once inside, she looked around. She remembered this house but now it seemed smaller than before. It was an A-frame cabin with a backside made of windows that faced the lake. Dark beams ran the length of the lighter wooden ceiling, making it rustic but homey.

A deck off the back had a chaise lounge and a couple of Adirondack chairs flanked by side tables. Beyond the deck was a sandy beach and the water. Seeing it gave her a chill that ran up her spine.

She moved farther inside the room. Overstuffed leather furniture sat in a U shape around a large wooden coffee table. Everything faced the window and a fireplace tucked into the corner of the room. If there was a television, she didn't see it, but then again, her family wasn't the television sort. They were bibliophiles and workaholics. She was certain when Uncle Frank was in residence, all he did was read legal briefs.

She went back to the car to get her bag of groceries and Z's dog food.

"As soon as you eat, you can play."

Beth had asked her if she was a mom. Laughter left her lips. She sure sounded like a mom. God help her if she ever sounded like her mom.

She poured Z a bowl of kibble, opened one bottle of wine Uncle Frank had left for her, and went onto the deck to take in the beauty in front of her.

Z looked at her as if asking permission to explore.

"Go ahead," she said, and he trotted down the steps to the lake. He didn't run into the water but slowly inspected the shoreline. A bird flew down and landed on the sand and he chased it away.

As she sipped her wine, she thought about Brandon and where he'd gone off to. He said he was searching for something, and she hoped he found it. He also said he was meeting a woman. Could that be the person who wrote what was in the pink envelope?

Feeling slightly inspired, she went inside and rustled through her bag for a notebook. When she returned to her seat, she wrote the first line to *Love's Lost Flame*.

He was lost at sea, just him and thoughts of Pertussis Loving.

She drew a line through it. Why in the hell did the author want the girl's name to be Pertussis? It was a disease. Might as well call her whooping cough ... And Loving? Which she was told was pronounced lowving, but no one would get it. Sometimes she wondered if the effort she put into the books she wrote was worth it at all. Pertussis Loving would die a slow death on the Amazon shelves because no one would read about a woman whose name was like Typhoid Mary. Might as well call her Phlegmy Loathing because that's exactly what readers would feel.

She tossed the notebook aside and stared at the sunset shimmering on the glass-like surface of the water. It was the perfect time to reflect on her life. She was thirty-two and had no plan. Well, she had a plan, but it wouldn't go anywhere if her client demanded a swashbuckling pirate named Flame McHugh, who loved a girl named Pertussis Loving. What she wanted to write about was a real-life hero. She closed her eyes and saw him exactly the way he'd look on her cover. Brown hair and brown eyes, wearing a camouflage jacket with the name Fearless on the tag.

She picked up her notebook and wrote the first line.

We all say we're fine ... but are we, really?

Brandon Fearless stood on the side of the road with his thumb in the air but his heart in his stomach. He didn't know where he was going, he only knew where he'd been, and that wasn't a place he wanted to revisit.

CHAPTER SIX

The old man said to take a left turn at Lake Circle until he came upon a road called Heavenly Gates, which led him through a cemetery.

Death wasn't something new to him. He'd been surrounded by it since he joined the Army. You didn't go into a war zone and come out unscathed or untouched by the cold fingers of death.

On some level, his upbringing prepared him for all the destruction. His life had been a ticking time bomb since the day he was born.

The first week of his existence was spent in withdrawal. Somehow, Mom cleaned up her act long enough to get him back. From what he understood, they moved from county to county. Once their welcome had worn out in one, they moved on to another. He didn't know what his parents did for a living, but he was fairly certain it wasn't legal or moral. Somehow, the word grifter always rang true.

He trudged past the gravesites, hoping this was some kind of mistake—that Maisey had led him astray.

Was it that Bea lived at the top of the hill as the caretaker or something? Deep in his gut, he knew that wasn't true. As he walked up the gravel road, his eyes searched the tombstones for her name.

To the right, he noticed a row of Bennetts and followed them down until he came across Bill, Bea, and Brandy.

The last time he felt this sick to his stomach was the day he was notified of his sister's death. His gut gurgled. Anger, frustration, and stomach acid mixed together to send his intestines into a twisting death dive of despair.

He'd come all this way to get answers, and there were none. Collapsing to his knees in front of Bea's grave, he pulled out the pink envelope and read it once more.

Dear Recipient,

I know it's unusual for a donor's family to reach out to the beneficiary, but I wanted you to know a little about your gift giver.

They kept the registry private, and if this letter found you, it means I hired the right person for the job. A good PI is like a good bra. It's working behind the scenes, but it's holding up its end of the bargain. Me tracking you down could be considered intrusive, but on some level, you became family the moment the gift was received.

I thought I'd let you know a little about Brandy. She was warm sunshine on a cold winter's day, a flicker of light in a dark moment, and as sweet as Abby's honey.

She was adopted, but somehow, I knew she was born to be mine. Brandy lived fully, loved deeply, and laughed heartily. While she was taken far too soon, knowing she lives in others makes the loss bearable.

I hope that her sweetness flows through you. Smile more than you frown, laugh more than you cry, and give more than you take. Most importantly, have a long and fruitful life.

With love,

Bea

P.S.: Enclosed is a map. X marks the spot. It's where a new life waits for you. Never question fate. If this ended up in your hands, it's because it was meant to be yours.

From behind the pink letter dropped a handwritten note from his sister.

Find what belongs to you. Don't stop looking. You know me, and I believe nothing happens by chance. I'm exactly where I'm supposed to be.

Love,

Gwen

His gut twisted, and bile rose like burning lava to sear his throat. He swallowed it back down because he refused to let it spew forth and desecrate the graves. He was a lot of things, but he was never disrespectful.

He stared at the pink stationery and the smaller white paper behind it. What did any of this mean?

She was where she was supposed to be? Dead?

He was here because of Bea, and Bea didn't have the courtesy to stay alive long enough to answer his questions. He was also here because of Gwen, and she didn't give him anything except the dictate to find what belonged to him.

None of this belonged to him. Not a single damn thing, and yet, he felt compelled to solve the mystery because it was his sister's last request.

He lifted his chin and his arms to the sky and screamed, "Why?"

"That is always the question," came a familiar voice from behind him.

Brandon hopped to his feet and spun around, fisting up, ready to fight. It was a rote response that he wasn't proud of, but he couldn't seem to stop the defensive reaction. He was fairly certain he came out of the womb ready to fight. If he hadn't, he would have perished.

Standing a few feet downwind was Doc.

"I see you found her."

"Why did Maisey send me up here when she knew Bea was gone?"

Doc moved forward. "Son, you're on a journey, and taking a shortcut won't do you any good."

"My journey has ended. It died with this woman." He pointed to Bea's grave.

"Did it? I've seen a lot of things in my life, and the most perplexing is how a woman who has been dead for years keeps popping into people's lives. Bea Bennett might have passed away, but she hasn't gone away. Her spirit lives on. I'd say she's more active in town now than she was when she was alive."

Brandon lifted the pink note. "Do you know anything about this?"

Doc stood in front of him, but when Brandon offered him the note, he didn't take it.

"I've delivered dozens of those myself, but I'm guessing that one wasn't from me."

"No, sir. This one came to my sister." He wasn't a man who let emotions overwhelm him, but he was exhausted both from the loss of his only living relative and the trip. He did it on foot because he needed the time to process, and the only thing he came up with on the way was that the universe hated him.

A rogue tear slid down his cheek. He let it fall, but it would be the only one he would allow.

"And you're here instead of her because?"

His head dropped so hard the vertebrae in his neck popped. "She's dead."

"I see." He pointed to a nearby bench. "Have a seat, son."

Brandon moved to the bench and sat on the cold, hard surface. The iciness of the metal seeped into him, causing a chill to move through his flesh and settle into his bones.

"I don't understand any of it," he said, trying to get the tremble in his voice to stop.

"Me either, so let's start from the beginning."

He wasn't much of a sharer. Most would call him a lone wolf. He was friendly to all but kept his distance. In his experience, the more people he allowed into his inner circle, the more vulnerable he became. Weakness was for the weak. That was something he'd never be.

Despite his desire to keep things to himself, he found the words spilling from his lips like water from an overfilled dam.

Doc sat there listening as he talked about his childhood, his sister, rehab, the Army, and death. The death of so many dreams.

He and Gwen had agreed to start their own families, and they'd be the patriarchs. Everything was supposed to start with them, but she abandoned him before they even began.

"You listen here, son. We don't get to choose when we're born or when we die. But we get to decide how we live."

He leaned forward, resting his elbows on his knees. "Don't the choices we make influence the latter? My sister was a drug addict."

Doc rubbed his bristly jaw. "I've been a doctor for a long time, and in my years of experience, your sister would have never been considered a candidate for Brandy's organs if she had an ongoing problem with drugs."

"But they gave her opioids for pain."

"Did they?"

He wasn't sure, but it was all he could figure out. It was the simplest explanation. That she got the transplant and started taking drugs again. He couldn't explain her passing a drug test to get an organ, but nothing made sense to him. He was grasping at straws.

"Was there an autopsy?"

"Yes, and they said she died from liver failure because of toxicity buildup."

"I see."

"Do you? I came here because of this." He waved the pink paper in front of Doc. "It says X marks the spot." He shrugged. "But the spot for what?"

Doc reached out and took the page. "Looks to me like she's guiding you to something."

"What's the point? Even if there was something there, I have no one to share it with."

"You're never really alone. Even an island has water. We create our own worlds. How do you want your oasis to look?"

He shook his head. "I have no idea."

"Now that you're here, what will you do?"

"I'm on terminal leave which means I'm at the end of my military commitment. My plan was to get out and do something with my life, but I don't have a life." He ran his hands through his hair. "I'll probably just hit the road and head back to Dallas."

"What's in Dallas?"

"Nothing." That was the truth. When he cleaned out his sister's place, all that was left was the letter and a book of useless facts. He smiled at that memory.

That was their thing. They both found the craziest stories and useless facts and shared them in their calls. The last time they spoke, they talked about how rubber bands lasted longer if refrigerated like that was important. She should have told him she was sick. She should have told him she was using again because he would have gotten her help. She should have told him a lot of things, but she didn't. That was who she was. Damn her silence.

"Then it seems to me you've got time on your hands. There is one thing I love about this town, and that's how welcoming it is. I love the sight of headlights coming into town but hate the sight of the taillights leaving. Stay a stretch."

"What does Aspen Cove have to offer me? It's a blink of an eye town. Hell, I would have missed it if I'd sneezed."

Doc pointed to the envelope. "The one thing I know is you're here for a reason. Maybe it's the opposite and you're thinking backward. What if it's you who has something to offer Aspen Cove? You owe it to yourself and to your sister to figure out what that is."

"You don't get it. This was hers. There was something here for her. This wasn't meant for me."

"You don't think so?" He laughed. "You would have never ended up with that envelope if Bea didn't want you to have it."

"Now you're talking crazy." Brandon resisted the urge to roll his eyes. "The woman is dead and has no control over anything."

Doc smiled. "I've learned not to doubt how far love can go."

"You think Bea's love of her daughter's organs transcends time and space?"

"I know Bea's love of this town lives on, and that's all I can say." Doc rocked to his feet. "You got a place to stay?"

Brandon nodded. "I've got a room at B's Bed and Breakfast." He thought about the name and hadn't put two and two together. "Same Bea?"

Doc nodded. "Yep. In fact, the owner was a pink envelope recipient like ... your sister."

Brandon cocked his head. Was that what X marked the spot meant? Was there some treasure that waited?

"You think there is something waiting here?" He pointed at the X on the page. It was right next to the lake.

"You'll never know unless you stay." Doc shuffled toward the road where an old truck sat parked. "Come on, I'll give you a ride."

Brandon grabbed his rucksack and followed the older man down the path. He popped his bag in the back and entered the truck just as his cell phone rang.

"This is Brandon." He turned toward the window and listened.

The person on the other end coughed so loud he had to pull the phone from his ear.

"This is Sage. I run B's Bed and Breakfast. I'm sorry, but I have to cancel your reservation."

"You what?"

She coughed again and continued. "I'm sick, and so is my husband, and the baby. I'm sorry, but I don't want to expose you to the crud."

"The crud? Is that a medical term?"

"I have no idea what we've got, but it's bad. I'm so sorry."

He said goodbye and hung up. "Well, on to plan B. Can you drop me off at the highway? My lodging plan fell apart."

Doc sighed. "Sage isn't getting better, huh? I told her not to go to Copper Creek today."

"You know her?" As soon as the words were out of his mouth, he felt stupid. Of course, he knew her. It was a small town, and everyone knew everyone.

"She's my nurse."

"Makes sense."

Doc headed toward town.

"You can drop me here."

"I could, but I'm not going to. You owe me a beer for listening, and I need a minute to find a place for you to stay. If I can secure lodging, will you at least stay a little while? I think you need to be here."

"Why here?"

"Because everyone needs to belong somewhere."

They pulled in front of Bishop's Brewhouse, and Doc exited, walking a straight line through the door.

Brandon left his rucksack in the back of the truck and followed the old-timer inside. Upon entering, his senses were hit with various smells like lemon oil and hops. It wasn't a bad combination, but not one he expected. Most bars smelled of stale cigarettes, fried foods, and sweat. This one smelled like pride. He knew the smell well. It was elbow grease and perseverance.

At the bar, a bubbly blonde bounced on her heels.

"Hey Doc, what's it going to be?"

"The usual, Goldie, and this here gentleman is paying."

She smiled at Brandon. "Sucker."

He chuckled. "Not like I had much choice. I was raised to respect and obey my elders, and he said I owed him a beer. Who am I to argue?"

"A wise man, since you didn't. No one wins an argument with Doc." She poured Doc a light beer and slid it across the bar to him. "What are you having?"

He looked at the hard alcohol lining the shelves and glanced at the beers she had on draft. "I'll have the same." His eyes traveled to an old register on the back counter where a cat sat swishing its tail across the keys. "Is that a one-eyed cat?"

She smiled as she poured the beer. "That's Mike and don't let him fool ya. He sees more with his one eye than you'll ever see with two. If you stick around long enough, you'll meet Otis. He's only got three legs, but he doesn't know he's different, so it doesn't slow him down."

Brandon picked up his beer and took a sip. He hadn't had one in ages, and it went down easily.

"Thank you. Best drink in town."

She smiled. "I'll let the boss know. That is, once he gets over the crud."

He raised his brow and glanced at Doc, who was talking on his phone—a flip phone that had seen better days.

"Does your boss happen to be married to Sage?"

"How'd you know?"

"Just a lucky guess."

"You're new in town. What brings you here?"

He gulped his beer and set the frosted mug down. "It's not what, but who? Turns out Bea Bennett summoned me in a roundabout way."

Her mouth fell open. "You too?"

"Too? You mean you got a pink letter too?"

She shook her head. "No, poor decisions and desperation led me to Aspen Cove. My story starts with a lie and a wedding dress."

He took another gulp. "Wow, I think I'd rather have a pink envelope."

She giggled. "I don't know. Things didn't end too badly for me. I got more than I bargained for, and so much more than I deserve, but I'm selfish that way, and I'm not giving anything back." She leaned in. "Can I give you some advice?"

He shrugged. "Sure, lay it on me."

"This town has its own way. You can fight it, or you can just let its warmth wash over you. I'd say, see what happens and where it takes you."

Brandon wasn't a leaf in the wind. He was the wind, but he was tired and maybe a rest was warranted.

Doc closed his phone and smiled. "I got you a place. You'll be staying next door to the bed-and-breakfast. Same arrangements. You'll have your own room, but you'll share all common areas like the kitchen. That will work for the time being. I've been told there is a gaggle of girls arriving that might displace you, but for now, you've got a bed for your bones and a roof over your head. I can talk to Jewel about the studio above The Corner Store or to Katie about the apartment she's got above the bakery when the current arrangement no longer works."

"Oooh." Goldie wiggled like she had a chill. "Lake property is the best. I'd say lady luck is shining on you."

He didn't say that he was supposed to be staying at her boss's place, which was also lake property. Pointing that out would only make him seem mean and her mindless.

"Lady Luck doesn't visit me often." He couldn't remember the last time he got lucky, and then a thought ran through his head. Every day he was in a war zone and lived made him lucky. How easy it was to forget one's blessings.

"Then you need a change," Goldie said.

Doc guzzled his beer until the mug was empty. "Are you ready?"

CHAPTER SEVEN

The trill of her phone moved her straight out of creative nirvana and planted her back into reality hell.

She glanced down at the phone sitting on her lap and sighed. "Uncle Frank," she murmured.

She put a smile on her face, even though no one was watching. Her mother always said it softened the voice and made it more friendly.

"Hello, Uncle Frank."

"Reese, glad you made it. Are you digging in already?"

She looked at her notebook and the opening paragraph she'd written.

"I was doing a warm-up exercise." She picked up the glass of wine and took a sip. "Thanks for the vino."

"You're very welcome. Umm ..."

She didn't like that umm because, in her experience, an umm was followed by a complication. And this was Uncle Frank who was a lawyer, and they didn't umm. They were decisive by nature.

"Was there something else you n-needed?" If not, she would get back to work, or something that resembled work. Maybe she needed to flesh out the character profiles to get her mojo going.

"When are your friends coming?"

Reese took a deep breath. If that's all he needed to know, then things were fine.

"S-s-oon," she lied with a big smile on her face. She hoped the smile made her sound more honest. It wasn't hard to fib to Frank, they didn't have a relationship built on that. He was a lawyer, and she'd been cheating him at cards and chess since she could play. It was kind of a dance they did.

"How soon?"

She tossed the notebook aside and stood before pacing the deck in front of the wall of glass.

"It's fluid. They'll c-c-call when they're on their w-way."

There was a moment of silence before he cleared his throat.

"So, you're alone now, and probably for a few days? If my spidey sense is correct, there are no friends coming, you just wanted to be alone."

It wasn't in her nature to lie so she ended up conceding with a half-truth. "Yes, I don't know when or if they're coming. Schedules are hard to coordinate."

"Perfect. I hate to inconvenience you, but Doc needed a favor, and I told him his friend could have one room for a few days."

"You what?" Her voice pitched so high, Z covered his ears with his paws. "You know I n-n-need the quiet to write."

"It's just a few days. Besides, you've got the entire summer. Doc doesn't ask for much, so when he does, I feel obligated to help. You know, pay it forward and all that."

She huffed. "Don't talk to me about paying it forward. I did my share already. I was happily picking up groceries when the woman behind the counter went into labor and Doc enlisted my help to not only deliver a baby, but he made me clean up the mess, and believe me, childbirth is messy." The whole diatribe came out clearly, thank goodness.

"You delivered a baby?"

She laughed.

"I was more like the janitorial crew, but I got to hold him for a second. And I w-w-weighed him on the p-p-produce scale."

"Aspen Cove should be great to spur some creativity. You don't get that kind of action in Oklahoma."

She was sure there were babies born daily in her hometown, but she'd never been a part of it.

"You're right." She wondered if maybe she could make Pertussis pregnant and have Flame deliver the baby on the deck of the ship. It was a thought. But it was a historical novel and Pertussis would have to be a virgin ... heavenly conception? Nope. She was back at square one with *Love's Lost Flame* unless ... Pertussis was a pirate too. Now that was an idea to ponder.

"Anyway, Doc is on his way over now with the guest. Just give him the room you're not using."

"Him?"

"Yes, but I'm sure he's harmless."

"Do I need to collect money or anything?" Why not wear another hat. She could be a doctor by day and a slumlord by night. A giggle built inside her.

"Nope, this is a favor to Doc. I'm not charging him."

"Okay. I don't have time to entertain him."

"No one is expecting you to. And Reese?"

"Yes."

"Thank you."

She hung up and realized she'd gotten through most of that conversation without a stutter.

She picked up her glass of wine and walked across the deck. Though the water was lovely to look at, she wasn't interested in getting wet. She avoided any depth of water where she couldn't see her toes.

Tires crunched on the gravel driveway out front, and her time alone had come to an end. She hoped to heaven that Doc's guest wasn't the chatty type. She didn't need the distraction.

She heard male voices and Z's ears picked up.

"Yes, we have company." She leaned over the decking and called out, "I'm back here."

She turned back to the water, which looked as if a ball of fire was settled on top of it and slowly sinking into its depths.

Doc rounded the corner first, and she turned to face him.

"Evening, Doc," she said, keeping her eyes behind him to see who would show up.

"Reese. I don't have any more babies for you today, but I appreciate you being flexible about having a guest. I had no idea you were an Arden."

"I had n-n-no choice in being an Arden or helping with that baby. You're quite the b-b-bulldozer, Doc. All day long, you've been disrupting my life."

He chuckled. "You call it disruption, and I call it necessity. We couldn't let Beth deliver her own baby now, could we? And this here young man can't stay at the bed-and-breakfast because they got the crud."

"The crud? Is that a medical term?"

He rubbed his jaw. "It's probably a wicked cold, but I hear whooping cough is going around."

"Pertussis?" She rolled her eyes. "What are the odds?" She cocked her head to the right.

Z bolted from the deck, and Reese called after him but there was no need. Brandon Fearless came around the corner, with Z walking next to him. The last time she'd seen her dog look so happy was when he brought her a bird.

"You?" she asked.

He stared at her and smiled.

"You?" he replied.

"Well, since introductions aren't necessary," Doc said, "I'll be on my way. Lovey wants to watch *Wheel of Fortune*."

Brandon walked up the steps and set his pack on the deck.

Reese called after Doc. "You owe me."

He turned around and grinned. "I'll deliver your baby for free, and I won't even make you clean up afterward."

"Sorry for the inconvenience," her new roommate said apologetically.

She turned around to look at him. With the water in the background and the flaming sun at his back, he looked like a pirate who'd come straight from the sea. A breeze kicked up, whipping between them, and wrapping his cologne around her like a cloak.

This man would be trouble for her. How was she supposed to work on a book when all she wanted to do was watch him? Even the way he breathed was sexy. Every inhale broadened his shoulders, and it seemed as if the exhale slimmed his waist. It was obviously her imagination because she saw nothing under his jacket, but in her mind, she knew there were sinewy lines of muscles—what her writer community would call gutters. Hills and valleys waiting for some heroine to explore with greedy fingertips and hungry lips.

"Do you have a heroine?" she mumbled.

"Do I have a what?"

"Oh sorry, a p-p-preference for a r-r-r-room." That was a quick save, and the stumbling over words would no doubt leave him mute. That was the thing about having a stutter. People didn't engage once they realized they could be there for a lifetime waiting for you to choke out the next words.

She wanted to curl up and die in a corner, but there was no time. She had work to do, and she didn't have time to be embarrassed or ashamed. By next week, this man would be gone and while she'd probably think of him often, he wouldn't give her a second thought.

She waved him toward her and walked into the house. The open kitchen was on the right and the bedrooms on the left. She took the hallway and pointed in two directions.

"Choose."

He shrugged and went right while she took the one on the left. Hers had the lake view. His looked over the driveway. They would have to share a bathroom.

"Rules," he said.

She peeked out of her door. "You have some?"

He chuckled. It was a low, warm sound that felt like a heated blanket on her skin.

"No, what are your rules?"

She could already feel her throat tighten and knew if she opened her mouth, it would be a disaster, so she mimicked zipping her lips closed.

"No talking?"

She smiled and nodded.

He frowned. "Your place, your rules."

She felt awful silencing the man when he was so pleasant to listen to.

"No," she blurted. "I'm qu-qu-quiet." She shook her head. It was so damn exhausting.

"Oh, okay." He glanced at the glass of wine in her hand. "You got another one of those?"

She nodded and pointed down the hallway before going into her room and shutting the door behind her.

Why did the world have to test her so?

She put her wine on the nightstand and flopped onto the mattress. The last time she felt like this, where butterflies flew through her veins and caterpillars danced in her stomach, was with

Charles Beaumont. They were in the same technical writing class in college. Their friendship turned into more, and one day it went all the way back to his apartment. While he made love to her, he told her how beautiful she was and how much he cared for her. She opened her mouth to speak, and he covered it with his hand and told her not to ruin the moment with her voice. He was the last man she'd allowed into her heart and body.

She realized that Z wasn't with her and rolled to her feet to search for him. With her wineglass in hand, she moved through the house and found her roommate and her dog playing at the water's edge. Brandon tossed a stick and Z was happy to retrieve it. As he came out of the lake, Z shook and covered her sexy roommate with water. His drab olive T-shirt clung to his skin. Yanking from the hem, he pulled it up and over his head. Yep, the man had muscles. Even in the moonlight, she could see he had rows of them just waiting for exploration.

She gulped down her wine and looked at the darkening sky. "Why do you have to be so cruel?"

Her subconscious answered. *Didn't you ask for a muse?*

CHAPTER EIGHT

He was an early riser. The Army instilled the habit of never sleeping past six o'clock. After showering, he dressed and walked through the silent house. A hint of daylight peeked through the wall of windows as morning's first light reflected off the lake. A single bird swooped down to catch its morning meal and sent a ripple across the smooth surface, disrupting the calm.

That was how life worked, too. One day you were eating Big Moe's chili in the mess tent in Afghanistan, and the next you were back in Texas burying kin.

He checked his pants pocket for his wallet and walked out the door. If he remembered correctly, there was a bakery in town, and if he didn't remember right, he'd revisit the diner. Either way, he saw a cup of coffee and something to eat in his future.

Besides, he wasn't used to being alone, and the quiet house gave him too much time to think.

The chill of the morning air crept into his aching bones, giving him a shudder. He zipped his jacket to his chin and picked up his pace to get his blood flowing. The fast-paced walk into town took less than ten minutes. Nothing seemed open until he reached the bakery where the lights were on, but the door was locked. The scent of deliciousness seeped from beyond the seams. And rather than leave the alcove and reenter the chill, he leaned against the door and waited.

It didn't take long for the owner to open and let him in.

"What are you doing out there in the cold?" she asked in her Texas twang. Hearing it made him feel like he was home, and truthfully, nothing had felt homey for a long time.

"Waitin' for you to open."

She laughed. "I don't open until seven, but come in, and I'll get you a coffee." She waved him inside. "I'm Katie and you're Brandon."

"How'd you know?"

"Small town gossip. It travels faster than a fart in the wind, I tell ya."

He laughed as he walked inside. "What's cookin'? It smells good." His own drawl sprang to life.

"Friday is raspberry muffin day, but I got some brownies baking too." She moved behind the counter and put a k-cup in the maker and pressed start. "If you want a raspberry muffin from the first round, you better put dibs on one now, because Sheriff Cooper has been cleaning me out on Fridays since the day I came to Aspen Cove."

He held up his hands as if in surrender. "I may not be the sharpest tool in the shed, but even I know you don't mess with the law, and you don't take what's not yours. It seems to me if I put dibs as you say on a raspberry muffin, I'd be doing both at the same time. I'll have a brownie."

The Keurig sputtered to a stop, and she turned around and handed him the cup of coffee. "I'd say you're pretty sharp for a Texan. Then again, we make 'em smarter in the Lone Star State."

He took his coffee to a seat under a board labeled The Wishing Wall.

"How'd you know?"

She gave him an all-teeth Texan smile. "You can take the boy out of Texas, but you can't take the Texan out of the boy." She held up a finger as if to say hold on a second and disappeared into the back. She came out with a muffin on a plate.

"This is from yesterday, but it's still yummy. It's poppy seed." She looked at his jacket. "I'm told you can test positive for drugs, but I don't believe it."

"Funny fact about poppy seeds is they do contain the same opioid residue that's found in morphine, codeine, and heroin. Though poppy seeds go through a thorough cleaning before they are ready for consumer use, they can still have traces of opiate residue. It's not enough to get you high, but it's enough to produce false positive drug tests."

She frowned. "And I thought my husband was pulling my leg. He used to be Army too but was medically discharged."

"A lot of good men were let go."

She looked at the timer on the oven and put another cup of coffee on to brew. "What about you? What brings you here?"

He leaned back in the metal chair. "You already know. It's a small town, remember?"

She sighed and picked up her cup of coffee. "I know you've got a pink letter."

"See, that's all you need to know."

She took the seat across from him.

"Is that because it's all you want to tell me?"

He shook his head. "Nope. It's all I know."

She waved her hand like a game show host. "I got this place by a pink letter."

Doc had mentioned Sage and the bed-and-breakfast but not the bakery.

"Did you know Bea?"

She cupped her mug with both hands and lifted it to her mouth. After a sip, she set it down. "Oh, I know her well, but I've never met her."

He thought he'd heard her wrong. "How's that?" She pointed to a frame across the room. "That's my pink letter. It was quite cryptic. Bea doesn't make it easy for you. She plants you somewhere and from there it's your job to make sense of it. She gave me a bakery, and I'd never cooked a thing in my life. I didn't have a dime to my name, and I didn't know why she thought I had a good heart." She blushed. "I'm not the sharpest tool in the shed, because if I had been, I would have figured out quickly that I had her daughter's heart."

He stood and went to the framed letter. In it, it listed a hundred reasons Katie deserved the bakery.

Joyful to be around
Pretty smile
Resilient
A good heart

He pulled his sister's letter from his pocket and when he returned to the table, he set it down in front of her.

"Do you mind?" she asked, with her hand hovering over the envelope.

"No, maybe you can make sense of it." While she read, he ate the muffin. There was no worry about a positive drug test for him. He was on terminal leave. There was nothing left to do but wait for the time to run out.

He looked around the bakery at the iron tables and the cross-stitch pictures on the wall. There were seven pictures of muffins, each labeled with a day. He needed to make sure he was here on Sunday to get a banana walnut muffin, which was his favorite.

She set the page down after she finished reading. "Not much to go on but she obviously wanted you here."

He shook his head. "Not me, but my sister."

Katie's head dropped. "I'm sorry for your loss, but no matter who got you here, this is a great place to be."

"It's good for now."

She pointed out the window. "Everything you need is right here."

He folded the letter and tucked it back into his pocket. "I need answers."

She covered his hand with hers. "Oh, you'll get them. The tricky part is asking the right questions."

"I need to know why Bea wanted my sister here. Was it some morbid attempt to get her daughter back piece by piece?"

Katie's eyes widened. "I never thought of that, but I don't see that happening."

"Because you know her so well."

Katie smiled. "Yes. Let me tell you what I know about Bea Bennett. She was never concerned for herself. Everything she had she gave to those around her. Even in her loss, she gave her daughter's organs. Imagine what that had to be like. Her daughter was dead, and I'm sure a part of her died that day, too, and yet she gave what she could so others could live. People like your sister."

"Okay, I imagine you're right. I wish she was here. I would have liked to meet her."

The timer on the oven went off. "Stick around and you will. There's a piece of Bea in everyone here." She rounded the counter and pulled out the trays of muffins. They smelled heavenly. It was as if the scent of them moved like a hand down the street to drag the sheriff into the shop because seconds after the timer sounded, he was at the door knocking.

"Would you mind letting him in?"

Brandon opened the door for the man in uniform.

"New greeter?" the sheriff asked.

Brandon offered his hand. "I'm Brandon Fearless. It's a pleasure to meet you."

"They just came out of the oven. I'm boxing them up now." She looked over her shoulder. "How's Merrick holding up?"

"He's as nervous as a cat in a dog pound. Can't sit still and the moment the phone rings, he jumps, thinking it's Deanna. I told him to stay home."

She giggled. "I remember a certain sheriff who also was nervous when he was expecting Logan."

"Guilty as charged."

She closed up the pink bakery box and passed it over the counter.

The sheriff held the box to his nose. "This is why I can't take off that last ten pounds."

Katie laughed. "Marina likes those ten pounds."

The sheriff looked at Brandon. "Have you had a raspberry muffin yet?"

He shook his head. "No sir, they were all spoken for."

The sheriff frowned and opened the box. "Don't let me stand between you and a taste of heaven." He reached inside and grabbed a single muffin and passed it to him. "Enjoy and welcome to Aspen Cove." The sheriff was gone as quickly as he came.

Brandon sat back at the table under The Wishing Wall.

"Tell me about this."

Katie loaded the case with cookies and brownies and other confections that seemed to appear out of thin air.

"It's exactly what it says. It's a wishing wall. Kind of like a wishing well, but we use stickies instead of pennies. Just write something you want or need and post it. You'd be surprised at how effective it is."

While she went back to work, he peeled the paper from the raspberry muffin and took a bite. The sheriff was right. It was a taste of heaven, which was a pleasant change from his living hell.

Nothing in his life was simple. And he wasn't one to play silly games. He thought back to the one thing he remembered his father saying when he was a child. They were at the store, and he saw they had his favorite candy bar. He told his father he wanted it and his dad said, "Want in one hand and shit in the other and see what fills up faster." He never asked for anything else.

Writing anything on a silly wall kind of felt like asking for the candy bar, but he did it anyway. He pulled down a sticky note and wrote one word on it: *Why?*

CHAPTER NINE

Reese woke as soon as the sun peeked through the blinds of her room, or maybe it was because Z was whining to get outside. She didn't normally lock him up with her at night, but having a stranger in the house, it made her feel safer to have the dog close. Tonight, she'd let him have the run of the house, which meant he'd be able to use the doggy door in the kitchen.

As a writer, she wasn't set to a particular schedule, but she tried to treat her work like a regular job. Back when she had steady ghost-writing work, she got up at seven and was working by eight. She held herself accountable to a chapter a day, and if she was in the zone, she'd do two. Anything more than that would tax her brain, and she wouldn't be able to work the next day.

Maybe that was what killed her career. She'd written the most amazing book. In truth, it wrote itself. She worked on it all day and all night until it was finished. The words spilled from her soul to the page daily until it was done. She was certain she'd finally found her muse.

When she turned it in to her client, she was thrilled. She

wrapped it in a pretty cover and sold thousands of copies, making the New York Times Bestseller list.

While Reese couldn't enjoy the accolades, she enjoyed the work that came in after. The second book did the same despite sales being lower, and then something happened ... her muse was gone, and she couldn't produce at the level she needed to make a living.

She dressed and went to the kitchen with Z dancing around her.

"I'm hurrying," she said as she opened the lock to the doggy door to let him out. Rather than relieve himself, he took off after a bird. Once the beach was free of what Z considered usurpers, he circled a large tree. Its trunk and branches looked like an old, gnarled woman bent at the waist, who pointed over the water.

She stared at it for a long time as if it were an old friend she was trying to get reacquainted with. The familiarity tugged at her insides.

As if doing his part, Z lifted his leg and watered the old girl.

Reese turned around and walked into the kitchen. The house was silent, and she wondered if Brandon was still asleep. She still felt bad for the lip-zipping pantomime. If she were honest, she was saying she didn't want him to talk because if he talked, she felt compelled to answer and that never went well for anyone.

As the coffee brewed, she sat at the table that overlooked the lake and put her new project into perspective. Maybe it was the name that was holding her back. If that was the case, she'd change it to something else in the interim.

The pot sputtered to its conclusion, and she rose to pour herself a cup. Leave it to Uncle Frank to have the latest and greatest of everything from the Wolfe stove to the lights she could control from her phone. And yet, he still had an old Mr. Coffee whose body was no longer white but yellowed with age. And the dishes were Corelle, whose claim to fame was that they were chip-resistant, but that didn't mean unbreakable. If you broke one, God help you because they shattered into a zillion pieces. She only knew that because when she was a teen, she was arguing with her mother, and she got stuck on a word and her mom threw a plate across the room, telling her to spit it out. It hit the wall and boom—tiny shards of glass went everywhere. They were still finding them in cracks and crevices years later. From that day on, she loved those plates. It was as if they knew exactly how she felt each time someone picked on her. She shattered into a zillion pieces.

A knock on the door drew her away from those thoughts and led her to the door where Beth stood with her husband and the baby.

"Oh, hi," Reese said. "You're out of the hospital?"

Beth laughed. "They only took me there to make sure everything was okay. I told them I had the best nurse and doctor in town."

Reese shook her head. "Oh, I'm not."

Beth looked over her shoulder. "Can we come in? I wanted Grayson to meet you properly."

Reese felt silly for making them stand outside. The chill had burned off, and it was warm, but it was rude to keep guests on the stoop.

"P-p-p—" She sighed and shook her head. "Come." She moved toward the kitchen. "Coffee?"

The man who took up half the space nodded. "I'd love some," he said and looked at his wife.

Beth grumbled. "I'm off the caffeine. It's not good for the baby. What else have you got?"

She opened the refrigerator door. "Milk or juice?" She was proud of the way the words slipped out without a care.

"Juice," Beth said and moved toward the table like she was familiar with the place.

After the coffee and juice were poured, they took a seat and stared at each other for a few seconds.

"Sorry to barge in." Beth looked at the notes on the table. "I see that you're busy, but I wanted to say thank you for helping me. Not everyone would have done what you did."

Reese wanted to say that she had little choice in the matter, but the truth was she would have done anything to help the woman.

"Y-y-you're welcome." She stared at the husband, who she met briefly at the store, but she recognized him from someplace else. She wanted to ask how she knew him, but she was embarrassed to speak, so she kept staring.

Beth smiled. "This is my husband Gray. He's with the band Indigo."

That's why she recognized him. But now she had so many questions.

"Indigo is here?"

Gray nodded. "The whole band lives here. Samantha is one of the other women who is due. Deanna, the manager of the band, is ready to pop too. We are on hiatus but should be back in the recording studio by fall. That gives all of us a few months to adjust to our new lifestyles."

The baby grunted and Beth held out her hands. "Would you like to hold him?"

Reese stared at the baby. "He's much tidier today." She must have looked fearful or uncertain.

"Go ahead, he was born on a convenience store floor. This one is made from tough stuff."

She took the baby in her arms and the entire world fell away. For a moment, it was just them.

"You are such a handsome little man. Make sure you grow up and be a good one. Understand that we are all different, but we bring something valuable to the world."

"I couldn't have said that any better. Anyway, we wanted to stop by and say thank you and offer you the honorary title of favorite aunt."

A tear pooled in the corner of her eye. She had no sibling, so no chance of being an aunt of any kind.

"But what about your siblings? Won't they be upset?"

"I only have a brother, and his wife Deanna won't mind. She'll have her hands full soon. What do you say?"

Reese pulled the tiny bundle to her chest and inhaled his sweet scent. "I'm honored. But I won't be staying in Aspen Cove."

Gray laughed. "That's what we all say, and then we plant roots, have babies and build houses. What was supposed to be temporary turns permanent." He shrugged. "No matter, though, we will stay in touch. You helped bring him into this world. That's a big deal to us." He sipped his coffee and leaned back, looking out the window. "Is that your dog out there?"

She glanced outside to see Z running the length of the pier and jumping in. Bobbing in the water was Brandon. All she could see was his neck and head, but her writer's imagination went wild.

"Yes, that's Z and ..." How did she describe Brandon? He wasn't a friend or a lover, although she was fairly certain he'd be great at both. "And Brandon."

"Your boyfriend?"

Reese blushed. "No, h-h-he..." She shook her head. "N-n-never mind."

Beth reached out and touched her arm. "Let's practice what we preach. What was it you were teaching our son? Understand that we are all different, but we bring something valuable to the world. We value what you have to say. So, say it."

A rush of emotion swept over Reese. No one in her existence had ever asked her to talk, knowing what they were in for, and yet these strangers were staring at her like their lives depended on her words.

She inhaled. "B-b-Brandon is a guest of d-d-Doc's. Sage and her family are sick and d-d-didn't want him to get the crud."

"There is something going around. Let's pray we all stay healthy." She reached for the baby. "We should get going and leave you to whatever it is you were doing." She looked more closely at the notes that said swashbuckler and Flame and Pertussis.

"I'm writing a book."

Beth's eyes grew wide. "You should meet my mother. She was a librarian."

Reese smiled. "Oh, I have. She thanked me."

Beth stood. "She hasn't thanked me yet, and I'm the one that made her a grandma."

"She seems thrilled."

"Oh, she is, and so am I. It's the first time in my life that I beat my brother, Merrick, at something."

Reese thought about all the things she missed out on by not having a sibling-like rivalry. Maybe if she hadn't been an only child, things would have been different. Having more than one child often took the pressure off in some ways. All the dreams and aspirations a parent had for their child weren't set on the shoulders of a single person.

She walked them to the door and said goodbye with the promise to visit their home soon. She imagined that now that she was an honorary aunt, she was entitled to spoil her "nephew." She had to admit that if she could have chosen a sister, Beth would have been her choice.

She returned to the table and watched Z frolic in the water with Brandon. When they emerged, a scene came to mind, and she reached for her pen before the thought was gone.

Brandon rose from the ocean like Poseidon. He gripped his trident like it was the only anchor he had in the world. But then his eyes found her on the beach. She was the pearl in the oyster he'd been seeking his entire life.

Her hand moved across the page so quickly she was certain the friction would cause a fire.

"Hey," a voice from her side said.

Startled, she threw her body over her work like the house was under siege and she had to protect it.

"Sorry," Brandon said. "I didn't mean to scare you."

She relaxed her posture and gathered her notes. She'd never been embarrassed about her stories before, but something about him seeing what she wrote seemed far more intimate than usual.

"No worries."

He pointed to Z. "He went for a swim. Hope that's okay."

For the first time, she realized he was standing in front of her in boxer shorts and nothing else, and that plaid cloth clung to him like whipped cream to pie.

She wiped her chin to make sure she hadn't drooled. "Fine."

He nodded and turned around to walk away.

"Maisey stopped me and said you're in trouble." He looked over his shoulder, but she wasn't staring at his face. Across his back was a long, jagged scar.

He must have seen the concern she knew was on her face.

"Childhood injury," he said.

She shook her head. She'd learned to not point out people's imperfections. "Maisey's mad?"

"She says she expects you for dinner tonight."

Ahh, it was because she paid for her meal. She didn't know what compelled her, but she opened her mouth and said, "Do you want to have dinner with me?"

CHAPTER TEN

Was she asking him on a date? He saw the way she looked at him. It was probably the same way he looked at her. He liked what he saw, but he also liked the warmth of a fire. And touching the flames always got a person burned.

It was just a meal ... probably not a date. Eating alone wasn't much fun. Most people saw mealtime as a social hour. While he wasn't a fan of all of Moe's specialties in the mess tent, he did like the camaraderie of dining with his fellow soldiers.

Growing up, he didn't have much time for family meals. None of his foster families sat down to eat together. There were usually packets of Top Ramen on the counter and cold pizza in the fridge.

He didn't get the warm and fuzzy families that some kids got. He got the families that filled their homes with troubled kids. Each kid meant several hundred dollars in the bank account. That paid for nice cars, cool clothes for the parents, and nightly happy hour.

Once, he questioned his foster family about where the money went, and he was told he could sleep in the garage the next time he was disrespectful. Winter nights in Midland were cold, so he never asked again.

"I'd love dinner." He stood beside her dripping water onto the floor. "I should change."

She took him in from head to toe and smiled. "Wise."

"What time?"

She looked down at her notes as if calculating the time she'd need. "Six?"

"I'll be ready." He walked past her, but he could feel her eyes on him the entire time. He grabbed a change of clothes and entered the bathroom they shared. It smelled like her. She was a field of flowers in bloom, and once he stepped into the shower, he knew why. She used lavender body wash and some kind of floral shampoo. By the time he was clean, he smelled like a girl, but she was a pretty girl, so he didn't mind.

Back in his room, he pulled out the useless facts book, laid down on his bed and read about bees. He always found them fascinating if not a little scary. Such beautiful and helpful creatures with a wicked sting. Kind of reminded him of some women he knew.

HE WOKE to a knock on his door. When he glanced at his phone, he realized he'd slept the afternoon away. He never did that, but it felt good to finally give his body the sleep it needed. Maybe it was the sweet scent of lavender that relaxed him enough to fall into such a deep slumber.

"Coming." He hopped from the bed and slid his socked feet into his tennis shoes. He grabbed his camo jacket and rushed out the door and straight into Reese, knocking her back toward her room.

She stumbled and he was certain she would fall onto her backside, so he swept his arm out to grab her and instead yanked her forward until he held her firmly against him. He always felt like all women were a perfect fit for his body. He didn't have a type necessarily. He liked them all from tall and lanky to curvaceous and full-bodied. But Reese's body seemed to curve exactly where his caved and vice versa. She was like a missing puzzle piece. Knowing that thought process would get him nowhere fast, he gripped her shoulders and set her back a step.

"Sorry, I fell asleep."

She looked up and smiled before nodding and heading toward the living room.

"Ready?" she asked.

"You want to walk? I thought we could eat at the diner and then grab a drink at the Brewhouse. Have you been there?"

She shook her head.

"No, you don't want to go, or no you haven't been?"

"Haven't b-b—" She shook her head and left it at that.

He knew what she was going to say. "Then we'll go." He shrugged on his jacket and opened the front door for her. "I wonder what the blue-plate special is tonight?"

The sun was setting, leaving its orange glow across the sky. He had to admit that sunsets in the Rockies were phenomenal. They reminded him of melted Dreamsicles Ice Cream Bars with their swirls of white and orange.

"Did you know that the Rocky Mountains supply a quarter of the United States of America with water?"

She shook her head.

They walked from Lake Circle to Main Street.

"Have you ever seen a bighorn sheep?" he asked trying to fill the silence.

Again, she shook her head, but she kept looking at him as if she wanted to know more.

"Apparently, they are the unofficial mascot of these parts."

They walked the next block in solitude as he took in the surroundings. There were houses that showed their age. Not necessarily in the way they were kept, but in the era, they were built. The town had everything from cabins to bungalows to Victorians. All the streets seemed to be named after plants and flowers, with names like Daisy Lane and Hyacinth. And then there was Main Street which was a long block of shops from one end to the next. They crossed the street at the sheriff's office and passed Cove Cuts and B's Book Nook. It had to be the same Bea who sent his sister the letter. He was tempted to go inside and see who owned it and what their story was, but they closed at five. It seemed as if the entire town rolled up the sidewalk as soon as the sun set. The only places open were the diner and the bar.

He could smell the bacon before he opened the diner's door. It was obviously a staple food served in the place from the morning offerings of bacon and eggs to bacon cheeseburgers for lunch and dinner.

He waited for Reese to enter and let the door close softly behind her.

"Where do you want to sit?" He always preferred a booth. Something about the high back and the enclosed space made him feel … safer. He also always moved to the side of the table that faced the door. In his experience, you couldn't be prepared for something if you didn't see it coming.

She pointed to the booth they sat at yesterday.

"We're building a habit here," he said with a chuckle. "If we keep going to the same place, they are going to think it's our table."

She dipped her head, but he saw the blush before she could hide it. He took his seat and scoped out the place. It was a habit to take in his surroundings each time he entered. He had a few rules: Know where the closest exit was. Understand where the biggest and most dangerous threat would come from. And find at least two things he could use as a weapon.

The front door was the closest exit. The metal menu holder and his butter knife were adequate weapons, and the biggest threat sat across from him looking at the menu.

He knew very little about her, but something pulled at him. There was a vulnerability about her that spoke to him. She was someone who needed a champion and deep inside he wanted to be that for her.

Shoving that feeling aside, he dismissed it as misplaced guilt. He couldn't protect his sister so had he chosen a surrogate? His brain told him it was nonsense, but his heart ached at the loss he felt. Why was his life full of would have, should have, and could have?

"Hey kids," a woman whose name tag read Louise said as she strolled by. "What do you want to drink?" She glanced at Reese first and smiled. "I remember you. You were a sassy thing when you were little."

Reese pointed at herself. "Me?"

Louise nodded. "You bet. You were a daredevil. You were the one who climbed up on Bent-over-Betty and scooted out to the farthest limb."

Reese looked at Louise like she was speaking an alien language. "N-n-not me."

Louise nodded. "Oh, yes it was. You just don't remember. It's probably a good thing, anyway." She held up the coffee pot. "Drinks?"

"Iced tea," Brandon said.

Reese held up two fingers, and Louise dashed off to where a large tea container sat on the counter.

"Daredevil, huh?"

She scrunched her nose. "Nope."

"Bent-over-Betty, huh? I bet that's the tree in front of the bed-and-breakfast?"

He could see that her mind was flipping through a memory Rolodex as if to test Louise's information for validity and when her eyes widened, he knew there was a sliver of truth to whatever the waitress had said.

"Here you go." Louise slid two glasses of tea across the table. "Have you decided on what you want for dinner?"

He looked at Reese. "Feeling dare devilish? We could have the blue-plate special again. It's Friday and it's mystery loaf."

The menu said meatloaf, but in his experience, it was always a mystery. Moe's mess hall meatloaf never tasted the same. It contained whatever was left over from the week in it. He'd even found noodles a time or two.

"Two," Reese said. "And pie."

Louise wrote the order down and turned but swung back around to face them. "I'm told you aren't allowed to pay."

Reese raised her hand to object, but Louise disappeared before she could say anything.

"Tell me what you do."

She frowned and sipped her tea. Grabbing the sugar container, she turned it over and measured three heaping teaspoons into her tea.

They both watched as it sunk to the bottom to form a layer.

"Would you like some tea with your sugar?" he asked.

She sat taller and jutted her chin out. "I'm t-t-told I'm not sweet enough on my own."

"Liars," he said a little too loud, causing a few of the diners to turn their way. "Who told you that?"

Her shoulders rolled forward. "My mom."

He laughed. "Moms are a piece of work."

She clasped her hands together as if in prayer and looked to the heavens.

"You were going to tell me about your work."

She narrowed her eyes, and he could tell she didn't want to talk, but that was the point in coming to dinner. It was a social time. He was certain it was because of her stutter, but he'd rather listen to her stutter than to sit in silence. It was in the silence that he heard more than he wanted to. His mind replayed all the things he could have done better, and he was exhausted from hearing what a failure he was.

She took a gigantic breath. The kind that inflated her lungs to almost bursting, and on the exhale, she said, "I'm a writer."

He cocked his head. "Journalist?"

She frowned. "Romance wr-wr-wr—" She shook her head.

He crossed his arms. He didn't like that she felt she couldn't finish. "I'm not going anywhere. Finish your sentence." He might have sounded stern, though he didn't mean to. He wanted to hear what she had to say.

"Romance writer," she said.

He smiled. "Oh, that makes sense." He sipped his tea, which turned out to be slightly bitter, and he added a teaspoon of sugar.

Her brow raised and she pointed at the spoon.

"Apparently, I'm not as sweet as I should be either, or ... maybe it's the tea." He stirred and sipped. "Perfect."

"W-what makes sense?"

"Yesterday you asked me a question."

She tilted her head as if confused. "What question?"

He leaned against the back of the booth. "Do you have a heroine?"

He watched as the blood rose up her neck to her face, turning her cheeks the same color as her pretty pink shirt

"You heard," she said with a hint of embarrassment.

"I don't miss much. It's my job to pay attention." He kicked out his feet under the table and his leg skimmed hers, causing her to shift out of his way. "No heroine for me. What about you. You got a Fabio in the shadows?"

CHAPTER ELEVEN

She choked on her iced tea while laughing.

"You know who Fabio is?" She was so happy the words spilled from her mouth without a hiccup ... or ten.

He grinned.

"Not personally, but wasn't he the guy who thought his career was over because he got beaked by a bird while he was on a roller coaster?"

She nodded. "Yep, but that w-wasn't why his career ended." She took a sip of her drink and followed it with a deep breath. "People are fickle, and they like whatever's bigger, better and bolder."

"Out with the old and in with the new I guess."

The door opened and in walked Doc and the woman he called Lovey. They went directly to the booth on the right in the back. Though it didn't have a sign that said it was his, the locals obviously knew it was off limits because no one sat there.

Louise walked over with two plates covered with meatloaf and gravy and mashed potatoes. A small section had a dollop of green beans drowned in butter. This was a heart attack waiting to happen meal, but she couldn't wait to dig in. She was starving. She'd spent the day writing several chapters of *Love's Lost Flame*. As soon as she changed the characters' names to Brandon and Reese, her imagination went wild, and her fingers flew across the keyboard. She spent three hours straight lost in the story and had to say it was the best stuff she'd ever written.

Louise stood over them like a mother. "Eat your veggies first."

"Yes, ma'am," Brandon said before he scooped up a forkful of gravy-covered potatoes.

Reese was always a good girl and did as she was told so she started with a green bean which was so yummy, she finished them before she went on to the meatloaf.

She didn't normally finish one thing before the next, but she did tonight. Veggies first like Louise said and then she devoured the meatloaf.

"Did you know that the first record of meatloaf goes back to about the 4th or 5th century AD and contained chopped meat and bread soaked in wine?"

"I did not. Why do you know this?"

He tapped his head. "I retain lots of useless information. Today I was reading about bees. It takes twelve bee lives to make a teaspoon of honey?"

She swallowed her meatloaf and gasped. "Seriously?"

He nodded. "I don't think we appreciate them enough."

"Agreed."

She scooped a fork of potatoes and let them sit on her tongue for a long second. They weren't the instant kind that were perfectly smooth. No, these had lumps that made them all that much better.

She let out a moan as she finished her first bite. "I obviously saved the b-best for last."

Louise came by to top off their teas. "You haven't tried the pie yet. We've got strawberry rhubarb today."

"Oh, wow." Reese leaned back and touched her stomach. "You're going to make me fat."

The waitress smiled. "Honey, when I was young and my man looked like him, I was skinny as a rail. Eat up. It's Saturday night and you've got lots of night to burn."

Reese felt compelled to correct her. "Oh, we're not—"

Louise winked. "That's what I said way back when, and now we've got eight kids. You'd think I was working here to feed them, but nope, I just need a quiet place to think."

With the jukebox playing Frankie Valli in the background and the low hum of customers talking and the clatter of silverware against plates, Reese would have never considered the diner a place of peace and quiet but add in eight kids and a husband in a home, and she imagined it was as tranquil as a spa.

She trotted off to help the newest arrivals—a couple of young firemen and someone in a sheriff's uniform whose name tag read Cooper.

"He's a nice guy," Brandon said, nodding toward the newest table.

"Who?"

"Sheriff Cooper. I met him this morning at the bakery."

"You went to the bakery?"

"I woke early." He pushed his completely empty plate to the side.

It was so clean she would have guessed he licked it if she hadn't been there to see he hadn't.

She thought about the bakery and a faint memory came back. She was sitting on an old metal chair eating a muffin.

"Do they still sell muffins?"

He rubbed his belly. "Had a raspberry and a poppy seed one today. The sign inside said tomorrow is apple spice. I'll pick you up one if you want."

She was so full now that she couldn't imagine eating a muffin, but she was sure she'd want one tomorrow.

"Deal. I'll make the coffee."

"It's a date."

He appeared so confident when he said those three words. Even though she knew it wasn't a date, a tiny bit of her wished it was true.

Louise trotted by and whisked the empty plates from the table and in minutes she replaced them with pie plates.

"Does anything come in moderation in this joint?" Brandon asked.

"It would appear not." She was amazed at how easy it was to talk to this man. He didn't shrink when she got stuck on a word. He seemed to lean in as if he were hanging on it and waiting with antici- pation. Not once had he filled in the blanks or dismissed her.

"You were here as a kid?"

The longer she stayed, the more memories she recalled. "Yes, the house belonged to my grandparents. When they died my mom and uncle inherited it. My mom hated it here. I think the only time I was in Aspen Cove was when I was about five." She recalled Louise's mention of Bent-over-Betty. "And I think Louise was right. I can almost remember jumping off the end of the branch, but something happened. Twice people have told me they remembered me and alluded to something. Like a disaster that befell me."

He chuckled. "That's a writer for you. No one says befell."

She sat up feeling indignant. "I do."

He took a bite of his pie, and she did the same. She was far too full to eat it, but it was too good to waste. When she got to about three bites from done, she pushed the plate aside.

"I c-can't do another bite."

He reached over and stabbed her leftover pie. "I can't let it go to waste."

"You're going to hate yourself later."

"I know, but I'm going to be happy now." He shoved the remaining piece into his mouth while a dab of filling oozed from the corner of his lip.

Reese wanted to reach out and swipe it with her finger but that seemed far too intimate. Then again, she wondered if it would taste as sweet from his lips.

Louise dropped off a check that had PAID IN FULL written across the front.

Brandon picked up the bill. "This isn't right. I didn't deliver anyone's child."

Reese laughed. "I guess you're guilty by association." She pulled a bill from her wallet for the tip, but Brandon shook his head.

"I got it." He left a twenty on the table.

Reese imagined if Louise had eight kids, she'd need all the tip money she could get. Though she said she wasn't working at the diner for cash, it was unfathomable how much milk and cereal a family of ten would go through.

"You ready for that drink?" Brandon asked.

She slid from the booth and swung her bag over her shoulder.

"I am, and I'm paying."

He had one of those smiles. The kind that made his face look friendly and sexy but didn't exactly scream smile. It wasn't a grin either. It was pure sex appeal. How many hearts had Brandon Fearless broken?

They left the diner and walked across the street to Bishop's Brewhouse. There was quite a crowd and she understood why immediately. Indigo was on the little stage playing an older song called "Empty Box."

Reese listened to the words and understood the lyrics exactly. It was how she often felt about her life and existence. She was an empty box but being here in Aspen Cove changed things. For the first time in a long time, she felt free and fulfilled. Maybe that was because things were working in her favor.

A tug at her elbow had her following Brandon through the crowded bar to a table in the corner.

"What would you like?" he asked.

She fished through her purse for her wallet. Over the din of the music and the crowd, she said. "Red wine and I told you I'm paying."

He gave her that smile again. "I always pay for my dates." He was gone before she could respond.

So, this was a date?

All kinds of things ran through her brain. If this was a date, did that mean he'd expect a kiss, or more?

He returned a few minutes later with a frosted mug of beer and a glass of deep red wine. They sat at the two-top table and listened to the band.

Reese watched Indigo and laughed when her overprotective husband stood like a guard at her side.

"Samantha White, right?" Brandon asked.

A woman sitting to the right said, "No, she's gone to the dark side. She married Dalton and her last name is now Black."

There was a racket at the small stage and Samantha let out a groan. Loud enough for the mic to pick up, "Honey ... I think it's time."

Reese handed Brandon his beer. "Drink up, because if her water breaks, I'm not cleaning it up."

CHAPTER TWELVE

Brandon did what she said. His name tag might have read Fearless, but he definitely had a few fears, like being the only one there to deliver a baby while being stuck in an elevator in a power outage. The chances were slim to none that would happen, but they could.

He chugged down his beer and set his mug on the table. "Ready when you are."

She finished off her wine and insisted on leaving a tip on the table despite him giving one at the bar.

"Someone has to clean this up."

There was no use fighting about it. He figured he'd find another way to do something nice. He was staying at her uncle's house for free. The man refused to take his money, saying that a friend of Doc's was a friend of his, but he wasn't a friend of Doctor Parker's. He hadn't met the man formally until the cemetery.

They weaved their way through the crowd just as Samantha let out a low but serious groan.

"Hurry," he said, putting his hand on the small of Reese's back and leading her out the front door. "Things are getting serious in there."

To their right, Doc moved forward with his little black bag in his hand. "Don't look, but Doc's on his way," he warned. "Just keep your head down and turn left."

She did as he said, and they rushed up the street. As soon as they were off Main Street, they were cloaked in darkness, and a brisk breeze danced off the lake and swirled around them.

He never took his hand off her lower back and he felt a shudder run through her.

"You're cold." He immediately took off his jacket and wrapped it around her shoulders.

"If you g-g-give me your jacket, then you'll be c-c-c-cold."

He lifted his arms like he was showing off his physique.

"I've lived through worse. This body is made for misery." While it sounded fine in his head, the words, once spoken, weren't all that good.

"Let's find you some happiness when we get home. I think there are some beers in the refrigerator, and I know there's wine."

He rubbed his arms and picked up the pace because while he wouldn't call it cold, it was a little chilly.

They got back to the house and found Z waiting at the door.

Reese went straight to the back door and unlatched the doggie door part so he could come and go as he wanted.

"Would he take off if you left that unlocked?"

She shrugged. "I think he'd come looking for me. Better safe than sorry."

The dog bounded out of the house and disappeared into the dark while Reese went straight to the refrigerator and took out several beers.

"Choose," she said.

He took the pale ale and twisted the cap off.

While she got a wine glass from the cupboard, he pulled the cork from the bottle she started yesterday. She seemed to like dark reds like merlots and cabernets.

As he poured, he asked her about the book she was writing. "What's your pen name?"

She removed his coat, hanging it over a kitchen chair, and took the glass he offered. She strayed into the living room and flipped a switch to ignite the gas logs in the fireplace.

"Fancy."

Settling into an overstuffed chair by the stone hearth, she sipped her wine. "This wasn't here when I was a kid." She pointed to a wall. "There was a wood-burning stove there. I know that because I touched it." She held up her finger and twisted it to show him the side. "See the scar?"

He closed the distance in order to see her finger, bending over to inspect the white scar. What compelled him to kiss it was a mystery, but he did. He cocked his head to the side to watch her reaction and when their eyes met, he thought she may lean forward and kiss his lips but a slash of white and black rushed between them and Z pounced into her lap.

Brandon hopped back and looked at the woman and her dog. The way she laughed when Z licked her face made him warm inside. This was a committed relationship. He took the space at the end of the sofa and continued to stare at them.

If humans were more like animals, maybe the world would be a kinder place. It didn't matter if you were gone five minutes or five hours, when you returned it was like they hadn't seen you in a life-time. They forgave practically everything and didn't mind if your feet smelled, or you fed them leftovers.

"Who needs a boyfriend when you have a dog like that."

Reese pointed to the floor and said, "Down," and Z obeyed, taking up the spot next to her feet.

She sipped her wine and smiled. "Well, as far as the opposite sex goes, he's been the kindest and most loyal. On a sour note, he farts in bed, and licks himself at all hours."

Laughter bubbled up and spilled forth. "Well, if we're being honest, I have done the former but never the latter."

She giggled. "Only because you're not flexible enough." As soon as she said the words, she slapped her hand over her mouth. "Oh, my goodness. One glass of wine and all the filters are gone."

He smiled because that wasn't the only thing that was gone. Her stutter was nowhere to be found. He'd like to believe that it was because she was comfortable with him, but it was probably the wine. Maybe when she relaxed, everything settled inside her and the stutter didn't surface.

"I like you filterless." His eyes wandered across the great room to the open kitchen where her notes sat neatly stacked on the table next to her computer.

"Before we took a seat, you were going to tell me your pen name."

She kicked off her shoes and curled her feet under her bottom. "I believe I was avoiding the conversation about my pen name."

He watched her for a moment and felt like if he waited just a few more seconds, she might say something.

"Okay," she said on an exhale. "I don't have a pen name."

"You write under Reese Arden?"

She shook her head, and he hoped they weren't resorting back to hand signals and head gestures.

"No, I don't publish anything."

He sipped his beer. "Oh, so you're just starting out."

She let out a noise that sounded like an indignant squeak. "I'll have you know that I've written two New York Times Bestselling Novels."

"But you don't have a name and you don't publish anything." He kicked his feet out and put them on the wooden coffee table. "I'm calling bullshit."

"No, it's true. I just write for others."

He'd heard of that before. "Like a ghostwriter? Is that good?"

She rolled her eyes and settled into her chair like she was prepping for a winter stay.

"Let me tell you how much it can suck."

She told him about the book she needed to write and how initially the characters were too stupid to live, but she was getting somewhere. Just that afternoon, she sent a couple chapters to her client and hoped that they were received well.

"Do you like to write?"

She nodded. "I do. You get to create this entire world and live vicariously inside it. Besides, I'm not really cut out to do much. Most jobs require a certain amount of verbal communication, and I'm not exactly good at that."

He lifted a brow. "I haven't noticed."

She laughed. "Now I'm calling bullshit."

He pointed at her near-empty glass. "Would you like a refill?"

She glanced down then shook her head. "Imagine what I'd say or do if I put one more glass of wine in me."

He grinned at that thought. "Yes, imagine. You might dance under the moon and skinny dip."

She finished her wine and set the glass on the side table. "No skinny dipping for me."

"Ever tried it?"

She rose and took her glass to the sink. "Nope, but I wrote about it once."

"Is there anything you've written in your books that you'd like to experience in real life?"

As soon as her cheeks turned crimson, he knew her mind had gone to the gutter.

"Oh, you write those kinds of books."

Her jaw dropped. "What do you mean by 'those kinds of books?'"

He'd rather show her than tell her, so he made his way to where she was. "You know, the kind that make your heart rate speed up." He ran a single finger across her full pink lips. "The kind where the hero grips the woman's hips and pulls her to his body." He did just that. "Where he whispers in her ear how beautiful she looked that night." As he leaned in, he heard her gasp, but she didn't move an inch. "Where the scruff of his skin is perfect against the velvet of hers." He rubbed his five o'clock shadow against her jawline and she moved her head to offer him more skin. "Where his hand travels up, skimming her figure."

"Yes," she whispered.

His hands gently glided up her sides to her shoulders. "Where he leans in and asks her if she wants it."

She lifted her head as if offering him her lips. He was so tempted, but he was also mostly a gentleman and if her filter was gone, then so was her ability to make smart decisions. Should they share a kiss, it would be when they were both sober and able to make wise choices.

He stepped back. "You write those kinds of books?"

CHAPTER THIRTEEN

Reese woke with the worst headache, and it wasn't from the wine. It was from Brandon. He made her want things. The first thing was to fist up and punch him in the face. What did he mean by "those kinds of books?"

She wrote books about love. Sure, this book was about love between a pirate and a woman with an unfortunate name, but they would fall in love and live happily ever after. She wrote about the deepest longings inside a woman's heart. To be seen and heard and loved and appreciated. She wrote about the things she wanted and thinking about last night made her want so much more than she had.

He made her want his breath on her neck once more. Those lips tracing the lobe of her ear again. His hands skimming her hips to her shoulders. Was it her imagination, or did he slow down just as his fingers brushed the sides of her breasts? He made her feel things that she had no business feeling—things she craved like attention and passion. He was like having a chocolate candy bar after three months of dieting. Eating a rocky road ice cream cone on a hundred-degree day. Feeling the heat of a fire after being out in an icy wind. He was the comfort she wanted and needed but did she dare indulge?

She rolled out of bed and into her fuzzy slippers and slogged into the kitchen where she found Brandon sitting on the deck drinking coffee. Her dog laid lazily at his feet as if he belonged there. Then again, she'd locked him out of her room last night because he kept whining at the door.

She couldn't blame Z. If given the choice, she would have chosen Brandon and the sunny deck over her any day.

She put in a new filter and some fresh grounds and brewed a new pot. It spat and sputtered while she waited.

"Hey," his voice came from behind and startled her.

She spun around and tripped over her feet stumbling to the side.

He moved so quickly, that one minute she was falling to the ground and the next she was in his arms with her head pressed to his chest. She liked where she ended up.

"You scared me half to d-d-death."

The rumble of his laughter vibrated in her ear. "Better half than a full-blown cardiac event. While I'm trained in basic first aid, I'm not the guy you want around when you have a heart failure."

Her heart was still beating fast, but this time it wasn't from the startle. It was from his proximity. She wanted to stay right there and soak up the warmth that saturated his T-shirt and breathe in the fresh air that had seeped into his pores. Instead, she stepped back and looked into his eyes. Boy was that a mistake. Those eyes were like looking into a decanter of expensive whiskey. They weren't brown as she originally thought but more amber with flecks of black and gold that gave them depth.

She took another step back and glanced at the coffee pot. She was terrible at awkward moments, and this was one of them. Did she strike up a conversation? *Oh, hell no.*

She pointed to the coffee pot. "More coffee?"

He nodded. "Yes, please." He reached for his cup. He must have set it on the counter before he rescued her. "I owe you some coffee." He rubbed at the scruff on his jaw. "I was wondering what you were doing today?"

She filled both their cups to the brim leaving little room for doctoring. "Working. Why?"

His head fell. "Right. Sorry. It would appear that my just hitch-hike to Aspen Cove plan had some flaws, like transportation."

She leaned against the counter and watched him. His face was one of those that only showed emotion when he allowed it and right now, he didn't seem to have his walls up.

"Did you want to borrow my car?"

He lifted his head and shrugged. "I thought maybe we could go into town together."

She laughed "We did that last night." She pointed to her computer and the pile of notes she had sitting beside it. "I have one of 'those books' to write."

He frowned. "That's not what I meant." He let out a sexy growl. "I was teasing you."

"I know. I get that a lot, as if writing romance isn't a real job." She stomped her foot. "Do you realize how hard it is? There's a story arc and two character arcs and don't get me started on subplots."

He chuckled. "I have no idea what you're talking about but that wasn't the teasing I was talking about. I was you know ... teasing you ... like in a ... sexy way."

He was flirting.

"But you stopped."

He nodded. "Yep."

"Came to your senses?"

"Yep." He moved so he stood in front of her. Not exactly in front of her but so close his body heat wrapped around her like a blanket.

"When you kiss me, you'll be sober and in your right mind. You'll do it because your heart and mind are saying yes, not the wine." He stepped back and smiled. "So, what about that trip to Copper Creek."

She stared at him, dumbfounded.

"You know, if you were a girl, men would call you a tease."

He shook his head. "I'd make a very homely girl."

She walked past him and out the door. "You're right. You'd be single and virginal like my heroine Pertussis Loving."

"Pertussis?"

She rolled her eyes. "Don't ask. I just do what I'm told." She took a seat and stared at the water. It was as still as glass with an occasional ripple where a fish came up to eat an unsuspecting bug.

Wasn't that the way of life though? Wasn't everyone a happy bug floating on the water until something or someone rose up to unsettle things? She looked at Brandon who had taken the chair beside her. If she was the bug—was he the fish or the ripple?

"Why is that?"

"Why is what?"

"Why do you do what you're told?"

She couldn't really say. She rarely questioned authority. She generally did what she was told because not doing so had consequences, but that changed the day she left Oklahoma.

Her phone rang as if thinking about Oklahoma summoned her mother.

She pulled it from her flannel pajama pocket and took a deep breath before answering.

"S-s-sorry, I f-f-forgot to c-c-call. It's b-b-been a b-b-busy c-c-couple of d-d-days."

Her mother huffed.

"You can't answer your phone?"

Reese hadn't noticed that her mother had called, then again, she'd been busy. Not only had she been working, but she'd also been ogling, and ogling required her full attention.

"Mom."

"Don't mom me. I hear there's a man living with you."

"Uncle Fra—?"

"Frank says there's a man there."

If her mother would just shut up for a second, she'd be able to explain. Hell, she shouldn't have to.

"I thought you were there to work."

She gripped her phone with one hand and her hair with the other and made a sound that was half screech and half groan.

Brandon's stared at her, and Z came running from the beach to her side. The poor dog looked at her like she was having a seizure.

"Shut up."

Her mother went completely silent. Sara Arden wasn't used to this side of her. Reese was quiet and compliant. She was a good girl because being a bad girl had consequences.

"Don't you get mouthy with me young lady."

Reese had had it. She'd been putting up with her mother for decades. She never talked back, but maybe it was because she couldn't get a word in edgewise.

"Who is this man and what are you doing with him?"

"What am I doing with him?" She stared at Brandon. "Let me tell you, mom. I pressed him to the counter this morning and had my way with him while the coffee brewed. And now, we're on the patio naked and getting ready to do it in front of God and country."

"Now I know you're fantasizing."

The fact that her mother didn't think it was possible hurt worse than anything. "No really mom. Say hello." She pressed the speakerphone button. "Brandon, say hi to my mom and tell her we're naked and getting ready to have hot sweaty sex on the back deck."

"We are," he said as his brows shot up in question, but her mother didn't need to know that.

"Got to go, Mom." She hung up and shoved her phone back into her pocket. She stared at Brandon, who was grinning. "Did you say you wanted to go to Copper Creek?"

He sipped his coffee and stared at the water. "I don't know. Is getting naked and doing it in front of God and country on the deck an option?"

She reached out and punched him in the arm. "I'll be ready in thirty minutes." She rose and walked inside but decided she should clarify. "For the ride to Copper Creek."

She went straight to the shower and washed herself of the embarrassment. How was she supposed to face him when she got out?

As she washed her hair, she realized she *had* mouthed off to her mother and it felt awesome. She also realized she'd had a portion of a conversation where she spoke clearly and with intent. None of it was true, she wasn't laying Brandon naked on the deck and riding him like a pony, but the visual was good.

There was definitely something brewing between them. Call it sexual tension or whatever, but something vibrated beneath her skin when he was around. He was a low-voltage current that warmed her through and through.

She hurried through her routine. There wasn't much she could do with her curly hair, so she didn't try. The man had seen her in her flannel pajamas, so wearing jeans was an upgrade. When she was dressed and ready, she found him on the beach throwing a stick for Z.

She loved the way he played with her dog. She'd once heard that a woman should watch and see how a man treated his mother, but she disagreed. Men knew you'd be looking for that. It was how they treated animals and children that counted. Especially how they treated them when no one was looking.

She picked up her bag and keys and walked out the door.

"Are you two ready?"

CHAPTER FOURTEEN

She tossed him her keys. "I'm assuming you have a driver's license."

He'd been driving since he was eleven, not legally, of course, but he got his license the day he turned sixteen. It was his foster parents' only gift to him. It was a gift to themselves really since if he could drive legally, they'd no longer have to pick him up at the sheriff's office when he "borrowed" their car.

"I do."

"You can drive then. My mother has got me all in a kerfuffle."

"A ker what?"

She opened the back door to let Z inside and looked over the hood of the car and smiled.

"Did I stutter?"

He climbed behind the steering wheel and waited for her to enter. When she did, he faced her.

"No, you did not. I'd like to point out that when you're with me, you don't do that much. Is that normal?" He rocked his head from side to side. "I mean, do you ..." He wasn't sure how to ask the question without sounding cocky or arrogant. "Oh, never mind." He put the key in and started the car.

"Wait." She reached out and touched his arm. "No. I'm a mess around most men." She shook her head. "Around everyone, actually, but with you ... with you I'm different. I don't know why, but I am. You don't judge me or rush me or fill in the blanks. With you, I can be who I am. I can be me." She sighed. "I don't think I've ever been able to be just me."

He laughed. "Overrated. I've been me my whole life and no one appreciates it."

"My mother hates me."

He backed out of the driveway. "You're not alone. My mom hated me and my sister so much, she traded us for a high and a ride out of town."

She shifted her body. "You're kidding."

He wished he were. "Nope."

"What happened to you guys?"

He didn't like to talk about himself, but he opened the can of worms and imagined it was only fair to let a few of them slither out.

"We ended up in the system."

Her hand shot out and touched his arm again. Reese was a nurturer by nature. He could tell by the way she took care of her dog and by the way she stuck around and helped deliver a stranger's baby when she could have walked out of the store and been done with it.

He liked the way her hand felt on his arm. The way the warmth spread through him, making him feel like somehow, he was important, and that he mattered. The only person he mattered to was his sister and she was gone. In the end, he couldn't have mattered that much because she didn't care enough to tell him the truth.

"Where's your sister now?"

He could have gone the Maisey route and said Texas because that's exactly where she was, but that was misleading.

"She's dead," he blurted.

Reese's hand left his arm to cover her mouth. "Oh my. I'm so sorry."

He took one hand from the steering wheel and scrubbed his face. It was still hard to say the words. But not saying them didn't make the situation any less true.

"It's why I'm here." He reached into his back pocket and pulled out the pink letter and thrust it toward Reese. "This was in her belongings."

He waited for her to open the pink envelope, but she didn't. Her fingers skimmed the paper as if she somehow knew what was inside was precious and should be handled with care.

"You can open it. I want you to open it." He needed someone else to read it. Maybe Reese would look at it and know exactly what it meant. To him, it was a wild goose chase. That X meant nothing if he didn't know what he was looking for.

She turned it over and opened the flap but didn't pull out the pages.

"I saw this the day I picked you up. It was tucked inside your pocket and when you fell asleep, your hand rested over it like you were protecting it. I was certain it was a Dear John letter."

He stopped at the highway and pointed in both directions.

"Which way to Copper Creek?"

She pointed right and he turned.

"I suppose it's that kind of letter, but not from a lover. Although Gwen was the one and only woman I've ever given my love to unconditionally and without reserve."

"So, the letter is from her?"

"Kind of. It's a letter she got from Bea Bennett, and then she added something to it. You can look. I can't make sense of it."

Out of the corner of his eye, he watched her pull out the pink paper and unfold it. His sister's white page fell to Reese's lap where she left it while she read the note from Bea.

"Wow." She ran her fingers over the handwritten words as if the feel of them would lend more credence to their meaning. To him, words were just words, but Reese was a writer and words were her lifeblood. "I remember Brandy. She was ... alive." She shook her head so hard she made a jiggling, jowly sound. "Well, of course, she was." She sighed. "There was Brandy and Bowie and Cannon. Cannon and I were like the annoying younger siblings. We spent time by the lake. My grandparents had this big barbecue, and I swear the entire town came over for my grandpa's hot dogs. He grilled them in such a way that the outsides were so done that they were almost burned but not really." She tugged on the seat belt so she could move a little closer to him. "You know when you go into a convenience store, and they have the hot dogs on those rollers, and they've been there for hours? The ones that are all dark brown and toasty looking? They were like that. So good. Anyway, Brandy braided my hair and painted my toenails. I haven't thought of her in years. I was here when I was about five and I haven't thought much about it since." She picked the letter back up. "I'm sad to know she died."

"Apparently, my sister got her liver."

"Can you imagine?" She turned so she faced the window. "I can't even begin to conceive what it's like to lose a child, but to have the presence of mind to donate her organs to those in need at the same time . . ."

He drove down the two-lane highway, winding his way through the mountainside. The road reminded him of how his life had felt since he got the call. It was filled with twists and turns and ups and downs. He was moving along, but he had no direction.

"Gwen was an addict." It felt like a betrayal to divulge her secret.

"She couldn't have been."

"How would you know?"

She pulled out her phone and searched for something.

"I wrote a book for someone once about the same subject and you can't be an addict and qualify as an organ recipient. I mean, she could have slid backward after, but generally, those who qualify for organ transplant have been clean for some time. There's no point in wasting a good organ on a bad bet."

He knew she was right, but somehow it would have been easier to blame the addiction than pure old bad luck. Then he remembered the autopsy.

"The autopsy report said she died from liver toxicity."

Once again, she was turned toward him with her hand on his arm. "All that means was her liver failed. It could have failed for lots of reasons. Why don't you see if Doc can make a courtesy call for you?"

He didn't know why it mattered so much, but it did. Maybe it mattered because he wanted to know that all those years he'd spent in the Army paying off her rehab debt weren't a waste. Not that Gwen was ever a waste, but maybe if he'd been by her side helping her fight her war instead of in a foreign country helping someone else fight theirs, she'd still be alive.

"You're right. I'll ask. What's the worst thing he could do?"

She laughed. "Make you live with me."

"Or," he said, "maybe you did a bad job of cleaning up, and he's punishing you by making you live with me."

"I'm an overachiever, so that scenario is impossible." She looked back at the pink letter and pointed to the X. "This is where Bent-over-Betty is. Do you think something is buried there?"

"Like what?"

She clapped her hands and smiled. "I don't know but I have a feeling we're going to find out. What do you say we grab a shovel and do a little treasure hunting?"

"It's not on your property."

"Then we do it tonight while everyone is asleep."

"Are you serious?" He'd done plenty of nighttime ops, but there was always an objective. In his experience, an X on a piece of paper was weak intel.

She picked up the white paper.

"Looks to me like Gwen wants you to find what belongs to you as well. Are you going to take the challenge, or will you let her down?"

CHAPTER FIFTEEN

She didn't know what had gotten into her. She wasn't a rebel. She was the silent observer, but after feeling the adrenaline rush this morning course through her veins, she'd be damned if she'd live her life on the sidelines any longer.

"You can wear your camo jacket. I'm pretty sure I brought my black jeggings and a sweatshirt."

"All right, Rambo, should I get out my camouflage stick and paint your face too?"

She hadn't considered it, but if they were going to sneak around at night then maybe he should.

"Did you bring it with you?" She waved her hand through the air. "Of course, you did. Be prepared, right?"

He laughed. It was a deep rumbling sound that made her insides feel all warm and cozy. The kind of feeling she got when she had one too many Irish coffees on St. Paddy's Day.

"I think that's the Boy Scout motto. I don't come fully prepared for war. Besides, you'd hate it. It's thick and harder than hell to clean off, and it breaks you out." He reached over and brushed her curls from her cheek. "You have perfect skin, and I'd hate to cover it with camo paint."

She wanted to giggle like a schoolgirl. He thought she had perfect skin. Obviously, the man had less than perfect vision or he would have noticed the crow's feet in the corners of her eyes and the chickenpox scar on her right cheek.

"How about we play it by ear and see where tonight leads us?" He pulled into the Target parking lot.

"You're no fun."

"Oh, I'm a lot of fun, but right now I'm hungry."

"I would have thought you'd have gone to the bakery."

He got out of the car and rushed around to her door to open it. She loved that chivalry wasn't dead. Lots of women got offended when men opened their doors, but not her. She was capable of opening them herself, but that didn't stop her from appreciating when a man did it for her. There was something about having a man want to look after her that made her feel good. It wasn't for everyone, but it was for her. Give her his jacket when she was cold? Yes, please. Open her door? Yes, please. Pull out her chair? You bet.

She left the windows cracked several inches for Z and told him she'd be right back.

When they got to the store, though the doors opened on their own, Brandon stood aside and let her enter first.

"What are we here for?"

"Food and coffee since I drank yours this morning." He picked a cart and strolled directly to the produce aisle. "You asked about the bakery. I walked there this morning, but it was closed with a sign on the door saying they'd be in later. Then I went to Maisey's, and it was closed with a sign on the door saying they'd be closed until Tomorrow due to the birth of little Ransom Black."

"Ransom, huh?" she asked. She had to log that name in the back of her mind for a future hero. It would make a good one.

"Movie stars and musicians always pick the most unique names for their kids." He moved through the aisle grabbing bananas and oranges and apples.

"How long are you staying?"

He glanced down at the fruit. "I don't know, but this will only last me a few days."

Her jaw dropped. "You'll eat six bananas in a few days?"

He shrugged. "Good source of calcium." He moved forward. "Did you know that a banana is actually a berry?"

"It is not."

He turned to her. "No? Then what is it?"

"I don't know, but it can't be a berry."

He added melon and fresh veggies to the cart. "It is. It has an outer skin, a fleshy middle, and an inner part that contains seeds that can't reproduce. A banana is sterile and simply clones itself." He picked up a basket of strawberries. "Did you know that strawberries aren't really berries?"

She shook her head. "It says it in the name. See?" She pointed to the word strawberry.

"Nope, they come from a flower with more than one ovary which makes them an aggregate fruit. I told you I know a lot of useless information."

"I find you fascinating." She picked up a basket of raspberries and put them in the cart. "I'll stick with these berries."

He laughed. "Also, not a berry."

"Oh my gosh. Next, you'll tell me that Pluto isn't a planet."

He turned the corner. "I'd fight them on that. I don't think it's fair to tell kids that something is a planet all their lives and then say it isn't."

She fisted her hips. "Then I'm going to insist raspberries and strawberries are berries because all my life I've been told—"

"Fine." He held up his hands as if to surrender. "You can pretend they're berries, and I'll pretend Pluto is a planet."

They moved through the food aisle of the Super Target.

"Do you want Cheetos or Fritos for our clandestine trip, or will they be too noisy?" She reached across the aisle and grabbed a bag of marshmallows. "I can get these instead. They aren't nearly as satisfying, but we don't want to get caught."

"Remind me to enlist you in my next black ops."

She tossed everything into the cart. Better to be prepared. They turned into the next aisle where baby formula was, and she rushed forward until she passed the food and reached the good stuff like baby clothes and toys.

"I've been dubbed an official honorary aunt. I imagine that means I'm obligated to buy cute clothes and stuff." She went to the end cap where the sale items were because they didn't call writers starving artists for nothing. While she had some money, it wouldn't last forever, but the little navy-blue jumper with the embroidered giraffe on the chest was a must have, especially at forty percent off.

"Sucker."

"I know, but honestly, the train has just about left the station for me to have kids so I might as well enjoy someone else's."

"How old are you?"

She covered her mouth with her hand in what she hoped was an act of southern surprise. "Why Mr. Fearless, a lady never tells her age."

"The oldest woman on record to conceive naturally gave birth at fifty-nine. Then there was a woman in India who gave birth to twin boys at seventy-four, but she used in vitro."

"You are an encyclopedia of knowledge."

"You're not too old to have children is all I was saying."

"You're forgetting something. A baby requires an egg and a sperm. I was raised by a single parent, and I'm not going there, so unless I can whip up some boyfriend material mighty fast, I think that ship has sailed."

They got to the hardware section, and she pointed to the batteries and wire. "Do we need anything for our treasure hunt tonight?"

"We're not building a bomb. Hell, I'm not even sure there's anything to find. Who writes 'X marks the spot' on a paper?"

She huffed. "Someone who wants you to find something. Don't be a quitter, Brandon. No one likes a quitter."

He narrowed his eyes.

"I've never been a quitter in my life."

"Don't be so testy."

"I'm hungry."

She took the cart from him and went straight to the checkout. When she tried to pay for the discounted baby outfit and her portion of the food, he insisted, saying he wasn't paying for his room so it was the least he could do.

"What about a burger?" she asked, pointing to a place in the parking lot called Tommy's.

"I'll race you," he said. He grabbed the cart and ran toward her car, riding the cart the last twenty feet, hooting, and hollering like a kid.

She laughed at his antics because it was nice to see him let loose.

Z started barking too which made it all the more comical. Her two boys were the highlight of her day.

She stopped dead at that thought. At what point had she begun to think of Brandon as hers? He wasn't hers in any way, shape, or form. Nope, it was a glitch in her brain. Just a hiccup.

"Is he coming or staying?"

"It's hamburgers. If you think you can keep him away, you're crazy. Have you ever seen that movie, Turner and Hooch?"

Brandon opened the trunk and loaded the groceries inside while she got Z from the backseat and put on his leash.

"Three times."

"Remember the scene when Hooch chews the seat in Turner's car?"

"Vividly." He shut the trunk and they walked toward Tommy's.

"That's exactly what would happen if Z saw us go to Tommy's and leave him alone."

Brandon rubbed the dog's head. "You wouldn't do that, would you?"

Z trotted forward as if he didn't have a care in the world, and he didn't because he was getting a Tommy's hamburger patty.

With their food in hand, they sat outside and devoured the burgers and fries. Each time someone got a little too close, Z growled.

"Does he always do that?"

"Yes."

"But he didn't with me."

"No, for some reason, he likes you."

Brandon smiled. "No accounting for taste I guess."

"Hey. He likes me too." She swiped at his hand, sending a French fry into the air. When it came down, Z caught it.

"Tell me more about what you do?"

He puffed up his shoulders and took a deep breath, "If I tell you, I'll have to kill you," he teased in a deep-voiced foreign accent.

"Okay, then tell me about that scar on your back."

He frowned. "It's not worth your time or my breath. How about you tell me why your mother cares who's staying with you. I mean, you are a grown-up."

This was the story of her life. Just the thought of her mom made her stomach knot.

"Y-y-y w-w-would th-th-think s-s-s-so."

"Stop." He held up his hand. "Nothing has changed. It's just you and me. You can talk to me."

She stared at him. Why was it her dog didn't growl at him, and she didn't stutter? Brandon made her feel like his last name implied —fearless.

"I can, but you can talk to me too. I know we don't know each other well, but you're asking me to share personal things, and you share so little about yourself. Why is that?"

She cleaned up the garbage and walked slowly back to the car.

CHAPTER SIXTEEN

He drove home, but the ride back was a hell of a lot less entertaining. Reese sat with her body tucked against the door as if she were trying to get as far away from him as possible.

"Look, I've told you more than I've told anyone," he said.

It was true. He wasn't someone who shared a lot about himself. He found that most people didn't give a damn one way or the other. When someone asked about your story it was a social nicety, but ten minutes later they wouldn't remember you unless you did something remarkable. He was forgettable all the way around.

She glanced at him for a brief second. "You don't owe me anything. We aren't lovers. Hell, we aren't even what I'd call friends."

He groaned. "Come on now. I'd call us friends. We've shared a meal and some stories. Hell, I've seen you in your flannel pajamas."

She twisted to face him. "Those are my favorite pair."

"I can see why." They had Malamute dogs on them that looked like Z. "Where did you get your partner in crime?" He'd always wanted a dog but never had a life where he could have one. They had a few K-9's in the unit he was in, but those weren't pets. They were soldiers in their own right.

"My m-m-mom is a vet. We t-t-take in a lot of s-s-strays." She played with the hem of her shirt, and he hated that she'd reverted to her stutter.

"Z was a stray?"

"No, b-b-but he was f-f-from an unwanted litter."

It broke his heart that he'd hurt her, so he reached across and took her hand.

"I'm sorry I pulled back. I'm not used to sharing. Like Z, I'm from an unwanted litter, and well ... we have a different way of fitting in. Lucky for Z, he got a good home the first time around." He thought about his life after the first time they were taken away.

"My parents were drug addicts." He squeezed her hand, and she tightened her grip. "I was born a meth addict. Gwen was born a heroin addict. We both spent the beginning of our existence in rehab, I guess."

"And they gave you back to your parents?"

He shrugged. "They say it's in the family's best interests to keep everyone together."

"When did you go to foster care?"

It was a memory he tried to forget. "The night my mother sold my sister for a high. Gwen was three and I was five. It was the night I got that scar. I'd always remembered useless information, but that night it saved her life and almost took mine."

"You don't have to tell me."

He remained silent for a moment. "I think I do."

She shifted from the door and moved closer, her free hand settling on his arm as if she was telling him he wasn't alone.

His grip on her hand was so tight, she had to know he wasn't letting go.

Reese remained silent. It was as if she knew he needed the time to gather his thoughts and his courage.

"Keep in mind that this comes from the memory of a small boy, but it goes something like this: My mom was shaking and coming down from her high. By then, heroin was her drug of choice. My father wasn't around much. When he showed up, it was usually with other men. I often took my sister to the park. It didn't matter what time it was; I saw how they behaved, and I didn't want my sister to see, so we sometimes spent the night at the top of the covered slide. But one night, when my mom took us with her to buy her drugs, she didn't have any money and some creepy guy said he'd take the girl as payment."

"And your mother was willing to give Gwen to him."

He swallowed the lump in his throat. "Yes. Drugs are a very powerful influencer."

"But to trade your daughter for a high?" She shook her head. "I'm sorry. I don't mean to be judgmental."

"Judge away. I didn't do it. The long and short of it was my mom handed her off to some creepy dude. I watched him carry my sister kicking and screaming into the house. She used to call me Brainy because she couldn't or wouldn't say Brandon. Anyway, calling that place a house was kind. It was a dilapidated trailer at best."

"What did you do?"

He smiled. It was a painful memory, but the outcome was good. "We drove away, but eventually I jumped from the car and got hit by another. The jagged rusty bumper is what tore up my back. I waited for the cops to come, and then I ran. I'd kept track of the turns on my hands. There were two lefts and three rights, and when I got there, I collapsed on the front lawn. I was a bloody mess, but I stayed conscious long enough to tell them my sister was inside."

She gasped. "Oh. My. Goodness. What then?"

"I woke up in the hospital with fifty-seven stitches but not one broken bone. Two days later, Gwen and I were in a foster home. I went to many, and she went to a few. I took out my anger in fights, and she went the way of our parents and turned to drugs. I found her in a crack house years later. I carried her out and put her in rehab."

"You saved her again."

He sighed. "It was the last time I could."

Before he knew it, they were in town. He backed the car into the driveway and carried in the bags.

"If you don't mind, after we put away the groceries, I think I'll lay down for a bit." Talking about his family always wore him out.

"I can get the groceries. Go ahead and lay down." In the kitchen, next to the kitchen table, she lifted on tiptoes and kissed his cheek. It wasn't how he'd imagined their first kiss to be, but it was a sweet kiss. It was the exact kind of kiss he needed.

WHEN HE WOKE, it was dark, and the house was silent. He stretched and groaned. Years of sleeping on cots or worse had put permanent kinks in his muscles and not even the softest bed could iron them out.

A glance at his phone told him he'd slept past supper and into the evening. It was already past nine and he wondered if Reese was in bed.

When he walked into the living room, all the lights were out, and he stared at the moonbeam slicing the lake into two halves. Movement caught his attention and his eyes followed it to Bent-over-Betty where Reese was hunkered down with a shovel in one hand and a bottle of wine in the other. By her side was Z who was doing his best to help her dig.

"Crazy woman." He marched outside and down the steps. He

would have called out to her but didn't want to draw attention. She was trespassing and destroying someone else's property.

He snuck up on her and just as she was pulling the bottle to her lips for a drink, he whispered, "What are you doing?"

She tossed the bottle into the air and the wine splashed out, coming down on her face. She let out a shriek.

"You scared me to death. And now I have wine in my eyes." She fisted at her eyes and groaned. "Now it's mixed with sand."

"Come here." He reached out to grab her hand, but she pulled away.

"No, I'm going to find your treasure. You need something good in your life."

She was right about that, but she didn't need to sacrifice her eyesight for it. "You need to get the sand out of your eyes."

She grabbed the hem of her black shirt and rubbed at her eyes. "I'm fine." She squinted several times, and he knew she wasn't fine.

"Let's go."

"No," she said so loudly that the porch lights of the inn went on and a man walked outside. "Everything okay out here?"

"Yep," Brandon said. He didn't know what to do, so he pulled Reese to him and covered her mouth with his.

"Carry on, then," the man said.

He knew he should have broken the kiss as soon as the porch lights went off, but he couldn't. She tasted like wine and happiness, and he hadn't tasted the latter in a very long time. Even the former hadn't tasted so sweet. When his tongue danced across hers, its velvety softness felt like home—like someplace he wanted to stay for a while, which is why he deepened the kiss and wrapped his arms around her so she couldn't get away. He'd promised that he wouldn't kiss her when she'd been drinking but shit happened, and apparently so did wine and this woman.

He pulled away just long enough to ask permission, after the fact.

"Can I kiss you?"

She moaned against his lips. "You better not stop." She gripped his shirt and pulled him closer.

"What about your eyes?"

"Fine." She nipped at his lower lip. "Totally fine."

"Seriously. We should go inside and rinse them out."

She sighed and sank against his body. "We should, but we're not going to."

He loved a woman with a mind of her own. "You're the boss."

She giggled. "That's something I've never been. Now kiss me."

And he did as he was told. He was used to following orders and hers were the pleasant kind. Under the moonlight, he made love to her mouth for what seemed like hours. He hadn't ever kissed a woman so thoroughly or enjoyed a kiss or a string of kisses so much.

When their jaws seemed ready to give out, he reluctantly pulled away.

"Wow, that was—"

"Amazing," she finished for him.

He smiled. "It was."

He took the shovel and buried the hole she'd dug, then offered her his hand and walked her back to the house.

"Why'd you kiss me?" she asked

He tugged her closer and wrapped his arm around her shoulder. "I've wanted to since the day you picked me up but ... I kissed you right then because you're terrible at black ops. If you're going to be sneaky, you have to actually sneak. The porch light went on and you were about to get caught."

She looked up at him, and the light of the moon caught her puffy eyes, but she was still beautiful despite their redness and swelling.

"I wasn't sneaking."

He glanced at her black clothes and shook his head. "Obviously, you were trying but failing."

She laughed. "No, they knew I was in their yard digging."

He stopped and stared at her. "What do you mean?"

"This is Aspen Cove. While you were sleeping, I delivered the baby's present, and then I went to the bakery to get a muffin. I talked to Katie and put a wish on the wall. Did you know she had a pink letter like you? Only hers is framed on her wall?"

He nodded. "Yes, but hers doesn't have an X. She got a deed to a property."

"True and some guy named Jake Powers got Brandy's kidney and opened the bookstore."

"He got a bookstore from Bea?" They walked up the stairs and into the house. He took her straight to the sink where he used a clean cloth to wet and wipe her eyes.

"No, he got a kidney and Doc talked him into giving something back to the community in Brandy and Bea's name. You see, not everyone gets something. Sometimes the people who are summoned here have more to give than to receive. Look at Sage. Sure, she got the bed-and-breakfast, but that just got her to stay in town long enough to realize Aspen Cove needed her. Now she provides medical care to the community, and she brought her sister here, who's a second physician and assists Doc. Katie got the bakery, but she doesn't keep any of the money she earns. She built Hope Park and grants wishes from her wish wall. Samantha isn't a pink letter recipient, but she is an Aspen Cove resident who came back because when she thought of happiness, this was where she wanted to be. She finances the fire department." She shrugged. "Probably a good idea since her manager burned down her house and nearly took out Doc and Louise's husband in the process."

"You learned all this while getting a muffin."

She smiled. "It's amazing what you can gather when you listen more than you speak."

"Tell me more."

She got another bottle of wine, and he opened it while she got two glasses. They sat in the darkened living room and stared at the moonlit lake while she spilled all of Aspen Cove's not-so-secret secrets.

She started at the beginning with Sage and Cannon. She then went on to explain how Katie had Brandy's heart and how Bowie had fallen for the same heart twice. She went on to tell him how Dalton had been in jail for murder, but the good kind because he was saving a woman's life. Then how Lydia showed up in town. Next was Sheriff Cooper and his wife Marina and how her ex-husband tried to kidnap then kill her to get his daughter Kellyn back. She took a breath after explaining how Doc's daughter had left for a decade but was back and married to a fellow soldier named Trig who had lost his leg in the war.

"I swear, I've got enough to write twenty stories from this town alone," she said with glee. "If I ever get writer's block, it's because I've simply lost my love of writing, not because there isn't anything to write about."

She let out a big yawn, and he knew the night had come to an end, but in his life, all good things usually did.

CHAPTER SEVENTEEN

It was funny how a kiss could inspire three chapters of a book and keep a grin on her face all morning. She had even turned the character names in her draft back to Flame and Pertussis because anyone who kissed like Brandon could be named whatever the author wanted, and it wouldn't have mattered. He could have been called Flicker, and she would have come running.

Sadly, when she came out of her room that morning, nearly running, Brandon was gone. He was probably getting his muffin fix. He had said he refused to miss banana nut muffin day.

She knew exactly when he returned because Z's wagging tail nearly toppled the dog over.

"What are you so excited about?" She bent over and rubbed his head.

She was excited too. If she wouldn't look so ridiculous, she might have wagged her tail end also. She got why dogs couldn't contain their excitement. Someone they liked was arriving, and it changed everything—at least the perception of everything.

Her and Z's day would be status quo until Brandon walked

inside, and then they would enjoy the feeling that came with his presence.

Rather than make a fool of herself, she took a deep breath and calmed her excited nerves. There was no use making more of last night's kiss than what was intended.

The soldier in him threw camouflage on a situation. That sounded reasonable until she reminded herself that once he knew it was okay to dig in the sand, he kept kissing her anyway. Either way, it was only a kiss, and she needed to adjust her expectations. She was leaving at the end of her three months, and he wasn't there long-term either. It wasn't time to order the wedding invitations.

This wasn't a book where she'd go to the dry goods store and find the perfect wedding dress tucked in the corner, try it on, and find it fit like it was made for her. It wasn't the story where they stood on the dock and kissed, only to have two rare swans swim by after a rainbow appeared from a clear sky. Nope, this was her reality. She was here to write a book. It just so happened she got a kiss as a bonus.

Brandon walked into the kitchen and held up a bag.

"I got you a muffin and a brownie and something called a snickerdoodle."

"You got me a snickerdoodle?" She took the bag and danced in a circle. It had been ages since she'd had a snickerdoodle. In fact, the last one she'd had was probably made by Bea Bennett. She opened the bag and peeked inside "You got a dozen snickerdoodles."

He smiled. "There used to be a dozen, but now there are ten. I ate two on the way back and they were good." He also held up the sticky note she'd put on the wall. "I'm returning your wish to you. You should have wished for something for yourself."

He laid the yellow note in her palm. She stared at the words she'd written. "Please help Brandon find what he's searching for."

He leaned in and kissed her cheek. It wasn't the kind of kiss she had last night, but it was sweet. However, that sweet didn't compensate for the sour she felt inside.

"You shouldn't have taken my wish down. It was my wish." She put the bag on the counter and frowned. "Why does everyone try to silence me?" She crumpled the note and tossed it into the trash can. "Why does everyone think they know what's best for me?"

"Hey," he said, coming to stand in front of her. "I'm not taking anything away from you. I'm taking the attention off of me."

She never thought of that. She didn't like being in the spotlight and never thought putting his name on a note would make him feel uncomfortable.

"I'm sorry. I should have asked. I was only thinking about helping you find what you're looking for. Have you ever been thinking about something, and it just shows up? It's like the law of attraction or something like that. I was hoping if we put that energy out there, maybe whatever you're supposed to find will just appear."

He set up the coffee maker and pressed start. "You want a cup?"

She nodded. "Yes, let's dunk."

"Dunk?"

She smiled and took a plate from the cupboard and placed several cookies on it. "Creamy coffee and snickerdoodles on the deck?"

"Deal." When the coffee was finished, he poured two cups and followed her outside. "Don't forget, this letter wasn't for me. It was for my sister."

She broke a cookie in half and gave the other half to him. "Neither was that cookie. You gave it to me, but now I gave it to you, so it's yours. The question is, what will you do with it? Will you toss it aside, or will you savor all that it offers?"

"I didn't come here for me. I came here for Gwen."

"Did you?"

"What do you mean?"

"Nothing. I'm just thinking about why we do what we do. Why do we make the decisions we make or keep the memories we keep? I think we go into things with good intentions but often we lose our way. I'm just asking if you're still on the path you thought you were on when you started?"

She dunked her half of the cookie into her coffee. On the deck next door, less than thirty years ago, she'd done the same thing with Bea Bennett, only she'd been dunking in milk. She remembered the woman fondly. If her memory served her right, Brandy came to Bea when she was a small girl, maybe five or six. Memories were funny though; she wasn't certain if hers were her own, or the ones her mother planted inside her head. You hear a story enough and you start to live it and believe it.

"Definitely not on the path, but honestly, I didn't know what I was looking for. I had a pink letter with an X."

"Okay, so tell me. If you knew then what you know now, would you have come to Aspen Cove?"

He was already shaking his head before she finished the sentence.

"No, like I said yesterday, not enough intel to make a decision. That X means nothing. I don't even know when the letter was written. Hell, the shoreline could have changed since then. And truthfully, I don't think we're talking about a buried treasure here. I think a nice old woman wanted people to know about her daughter."

"Maybe. But nothing has really changed so tell me why you came."

"Because my sister asked me to."

"Did you do everything she asked?"

"She never really asked for much. I tended to insert myself in her life more than she asked for my presence."

"Because you knew what was best for her?"

He dunked his cookie in the mug but left it for too long, and when he tried to pull it out, it fell to the bottom. He let out an "Aww," and let his head fall forward. For a second, she caught a glimpse of his inner child and wondered how any parent could have done what they did to him.

"Obviously not, but I was the only one who had her back."

A commotion came from the side of the house, ending their conversation. Several of the townsfolk rounded the corner with shovels and chairs, while others carried casserole dishes and covered plates.

Reese rose from her chair. "What's going on?"

"I hear we're having a treasure hunt," Bowie said. He walked up the steps and offered his hand to Brandon. "I'm Bowie Bishop." He chuckled. "Man, all I can say is don't ask questions, just grab a shovel and start digging. When my wife says we're fulfilling a wish, I just ask where and when."

Brandon looked at Reese like he wanted to bury her with one of the shovels, but she shrugged. "I guess you were too late." She tried to hide her smile, but she was thrilled the town had come together to help a stranger. Then again, when she walked around the day before, she was told more than once that a stranger was simply someone they hadn't met yet. As the beach filled with new friends, and the neighbors pulled up their barbecues and lit up the fires, this turned into more of a celebration of life than a search mission.

Z even met a few friends when Sage let Otis loose, and Katie brought Bishop out to play. Trig carried Clovis to the beach, but the overweight Bassett Hound didn't move from where his owner placed him, so Z wasn't interested.

Within an hour the beach looked like a scene from the movie "Holes," with mounds of dirt and craters everywhere.

Reese stayed close to Brandon since she'd been the instigator of this shovel shindig.

Near Bent-over-Betty someone yelled, "I found something." A

young man they called Basil held up something and a gasp came from Maisey. "Give that to me. That's my good wig." She swiped the sandy clump from the young man's hand and walked into Sage and Cannon's house with an indignant harumph.

After two hours of digging, and no one finding anything, they all sat down to eat. Tables and chairs appeared out of nowhere. Bags of chips, six packs of beer, soda, and plates of cookies seemed to magically appear.

"I told you nothing was there. X didn't mark anything," Brandon said.

Reese looked and smiled. "Maybe. Or maybe we all see things through different lenses."

CHAPTER EIGHTEEN

Brandon sipped his beer and watched as the beach went from a land mine disaster field to a smooth, ready for volleyball surface. Two of the younger firefighters pulled out a frisbee and started up a game.

He watched as a grizzled old cowboy kept his eye on what Brandon imagined were his daughters—two attractive twenty-something things wearing blue jeans, cowboy hats, and great big smiles.

"Stick around. I may need back up."

Brandon turned to see Sheriff Cooper next to him. "There's something about fathers and their daughters. I know I'd kill for mine." He pointed to the little fireball running after a chocolate lab down the beach. "That's Kellyn and God bless any boy who thinks he's dating her." He nodded toward the two guys on the beach, still in Aspen Cove Fire Department uniforms. "That's Jacob and James, and those two girls are the youngest members of Lloyd Dawson's Bouquet."

He leaned against the deck and watched as one of the girls dove for the frisbee. She took a tumble, and her hat went blowing in the sand, and when James went to help her up, the cowboy the sheriff called Lloyd Dawson told him to "git" his hands off her. The sassy little blonde turned on her father and ranted at him until she had the old cowboy with his back up against the lake.

"Not sure who I'd be more afraid of at this point." He stared at both girls. "Did you say bouquet?"

"I only know Poppy's name for sure because she's married to my deputy Mark, but there's a Daisy and a Violet and a Lily in there somewhere and if my memory serves me correctly, there's a Rose too." He pointed to the young man who found Maisey's wig. "That's Basil like the spice. I'm fairly certain he was supposed to be Mum or Dahlia, but probably surprised his mama and came out a boy."

"I hope he knows how to fight," Brandon said.

"Most cowboys do. He likes to go by Baz."

Brandon shook his head. "That would still get him an ass-whoopin' in the army."

"What did you do in the service?"

It was a question he got asked a lot. "A whole lot of nothing until something happened and then it seemed like controlled chaos."

Sheriff Cooper nodded. "I get it. If you told me, you'd have to kill me."

Brandon chuckled. "Something like that."

"You sticking around town for a while?"

That was the question that had been rolling around his brain all day. What was his next move? He didn't have a plan. He had a paycheck coming in for the next forty something days. He had money in the bank. What he didn't have was a clue as to what to do with his life. He looked around and felt envious of the people in front of him. They at least had a life.

"What brought you here?" he asked.

"I've always loved to avoid and answer a question with a question too." Sheriff Cooper shifted his body weight and crossed one leg in front of the other. "But to answer your question, fate brought me here. What was supposed to be a routine speeding ticket turned into me getting shot, and I decided I wanted a quieter life, so I packed up and moved to a small mountain town that was supposed to be serene and peaceful."

"Did you get what you wanted?" He raised a brow because he'd already heard the story about Cooper's wife and her murderous ex.

The sheriff laughed. "All I have to say is be careful what you ask for. The town is great, but it's got its quirks. The one thing I've learned is crime has no address, and trouble has a way of finding a home everywhere. You have to be willing to run it out of town before it plants roots." He nodded toward the man standing next to Maisey. "Years ago, Ben was the town drunk. Now he might as well be its mayor." He glanced at a woman who'd picked up the frisbee and threw it to another firefighter that had just arrived. "That's Maisey's niece, Riley. She's a metal artist and also the town's resident arsonist."

"What?"

"In all fairness, it wasn't her that started the fire but a jealous rival, however she kind of left herself open to it. Her husband is the fire chief, Luke Mosier."

"That must have been an interesting talk."

"Then we have Thomas, who is also a firefighter and is married to Eden. If you stick around, have them tell you their story, it's quite heartwarming."

"So, everyone here has a story."

Sheriff Cooper patted him on the back. "Everyone everywhere has a story. You have to figure out what yours is. Are you sticking around to figure it out?"

"Not sure, why?"

He jutted his chin toward a picnic table where a large man hovered over a very pregnant woman.

"The town is growing, and by the looks of it, my deputy will be on maternity leave any day now. I bet you'd make a great fill-in if you're interested, or looking for a job."

"I've usually been on the other side of the law."

"Perfect, it's good to have a well-rounded team. You'll have a very different perspective. Let me know what you decide."

He walked away leaving Brandon on his own to take in the town doing what this town did. They came out in force at the request of a bakery owner who wasn't even a long-term resident. They dug holes in the sand because a girl who hadn't been here since she was five years old wrote a note sort of asking them to.

It made no sense to him at all. Most of these people were virtual strangers. He got that family did for family. He understood that Lloyd looking out after his daughters was his job. Kind of like it was Brandon's job to see after his sister. But the town coming to Katie's bidding, and Katie caring about Reese's note? He shook his head. He knew that wasn't it at all. It was Katie caring about him. She knew he had the letter, and she was trying to help him, but she had no skin in his game. She could have walked away and not given him a second thought. Most people would have.

"Nice community, huh?"

Brandon jumped at that sound of Doc's voice. Any other time and the old man would have been heard with his shuffling about, but the sand must have eaten up the noise he usually made.

"Yeah, it's okay, I guess."

"How's the house?" He looked up at the deck behind them.

"It's been great, sir. Thank you for helping me out."

Doc smiled. "How's the host?"

Brandon felt like a teenage boy who'd been caught with a flashlight and a girlie magazine. "Reese is ... special."

"You know she nearly drowned in that lake."

"Really?"

Doc nodded. "I only met her the one summer, but she was a

daredevil. Her grandparents would spend the summers up here and Reese showed up that summer with her mom and ran around like her tail end was on fire. I swear she spent more time in my office than any other kid that summer, and that's saying a lot because little Bailey Brown spends a lot of time in my office these days. Those two are twins split by three decades and not related at all."

"She hasn't said anything about a near drowning."

"Memories are like that. The farther they get away from us, the more skewed they become." He pointed to Bent-over-Betty. "One day she convinced Brandy Bennett to climb onto the edge of a branch. Now Brandy was older and should have been wiser, but Reese was persuasive. She was convinced she was going to be the next Mark Spitz or somethin' or another. Anyway, both girls got to the edge and their combined weight was too much. The old branch broke, and they both went into the water, but only Brandy came out. Turns out that big ole branch cold-cocked Reese on her way in. Next time you're kissing the girl, check out the scar she's got on the right side of her head just behind her ear. I stitched that up myself."

Brandon stood there staring at the tree with the jagged limb that corroborated his story. "You know I kissed her?"

"Son, does a bear poop in the woods? Not much happens in town that I don't hear about."

"If Brandy was the only one who came out, who saved her that day?"

Doc shrugged. "No one knows. Brandy ran in to get her mama, and when they came out, Reese was laid out on the beach like someone had plucked her from the water and put her there. It's like fate had a hand in things. The very water that Brandy fell into that day, took her life years later, but her presence in town saved so many others that day. No matter how hard we try, we can't save them all. I kind of feel like sometimes we aren't supposed to."

Brandon considered that for a moment.

"Doc, can you do me a favor?"

"You'll owe me another beer."

"Seems like a cheap trade-off for what I'm about to ask." He gulped his beer and threw the empty bottle into the nearby trashcan. "Can you request a copy of my sister's autopsy and tell me if she was using before she died."

Doc nodded. "I can, but will it make a difference? Either way, she's still dead."

"I just feel like somehow I failed her in some way."

Doc looked at him straight on. His gaze was so intense that Brandon wanted to turn away.

"If your sister was using, then the only person who failed her was her. All we can do is go into a situation with the best intentions." Doc walked away mumbling something about youth wasted on young uns.

As soon as he left, Reese walked over.

"Sorry you didn't find what you were looking for."

His earlier response had dimmed her excitement, and he felt bad for that. "Are you kidding? Basil found a wig. I'm pretty sure it's mine since this search party was in my honor. In fact, I think I'm going to ask Maisey for it."

He marched toward where Maisey stood, but before he could get the words out, he heard the pregnant woman standing next to her groan, and her husband Merrick ask, "Is it time?"

From the deck, Reese called out to Doc, "You're up, Doc."

The old man smiled at her.

"You want to deliver another one?"

"Not on your life." Reese lifted her hand and waved before walking into the house and closing the door behind her.

Doc and the couple disappeared as did Elsa and Trenton, the couple he'd met that first night in the diner.

As the night wore on, the crowd thinned until only he and Bent-over-Betty remained.

He sat at the edge of the water and listened as the water eased up the shore and retreated.

"Do you remember Reese?" he asked the old, gnarled tree.

"I think she remembers you."

CHAPTER NINETEEN

Three more chapters flowed from her. Her client was so happy with the work she'd submitted, but the last round she asked who Brandon was because Reese mistakenly put his name in the manuscript instead of Flame.

Reese laughed. She didn't want to explain that Brandon was the true Flame and she had to envision every scene with the sexy soldier in mind before she could put the words down on the page.

She was coming up on the true bodice ripper scene of the book where the two would finally knock boots because her heroine was a pirate in her own right and wore them.

She stared at the lake and pretended it was the open sea. She could see the ship and its wooden mast. The smell of salt filled the air despite the water being fresh before her. Though she sat in a chair on the deck, the wooden planks beneath her feet rocked to and fro in her imagination.

She giggled out loud and let her fingers dance across the computer keyboard. She hadn't been this excited to write in a very long time. It was as if the words were battling to escape her.

Pertussis stalked him across his quarters.

"You'll have me when I say so."

Her breasts heaved from the thin lace of her chemise. The sun-kissed skin called to him like a mythical siren. Oh, who was he kidding? Everything about her called to him like the beauties from the deep, and like the mythical creatures, Pertussis was dangerous. Once he had her he knew he would fall under her spell forever.

"I'll take you when I want you." *He moved slowly toward her until they were face to face. He took a step forward and she retreated until he had her pinned against the desk.*

"When will that be?" *She taunted*

He reached behind her and cleared the desk with a single swipe before silencing her with a kiss.

"You look happy."

She jumped in her seat and slammed her laptop closed.

"Were you reading what I wrote?"

"No. Should I have been?"

"Absolutely not." She knew her cheeks were red because her entire face felt hot like her face had been dipped in fire.

He flopped into the chair beside her.

"Now I'm intrigued. Tell me about the book."

She rolled her eyes. Though statistically sixteen percent of romance books were read by men, she had never met one that fessed up to being one of them.

"You don't want to know."

He leaned back into his chair and stared at her. She'd never had a man give her all his attention before. The closest thing she had to that kind of notice was her Uncle Frank, and then he only paid attention in fits and spurts between legal briefs and phone calls. It was the only reason he thought she was decent at chess and checkers and cards. She wasn't good at all. She cheated, but what five-year-old didn't. When she was a kid, he would turn his back, and she'd swipe his game piece from the board. He wasn't engaged enough to notice.

"But I do want to know. Walters read them all the time, and I'm curious."

"A guy in your ...?" She cocked her head in question.

"Platoon. And while Walters looks like a guy, and for all intents and purposes is treated like one of the guys, he is missing what most biological guys have."

She narrowed her eyes and couldn't help but gaze down at his crotch.

He smiled. "Yep, that. Walters is a chick. Her name is Philippa Walters, but we either called her Phil or Walters."

"Is it weird having women in a combat zone with you?" She'd always wondered but never asked. Where did Brandon sit with his thoughts about women's and men's roles in the world? She grew up in a world that was ruled by women for women, and somehow, she never felt very powerful.

Her mother was the equivalent of a misogynist. It wasn't that she hated men, she just didn't see any use for them.

He rubbed his chin which had a shadow of whiskers on it, and she found herself wondering if they would feel soft or rough on the skin of her neck, cheek ... thighs. Oh my, her brain was way too active today.

"Tell me about this Walters woman."

"I have no trouble with women who join the service. Same rules for all apply. If I had any problem at all, it would come from a personal nature, and my need to protect."

"You have a savior complex." She smiled. "That's why you make an amazing romance hero." She cleared her throat realizing her mistake. She'd just inadvertently fessed up to using him as her muse. And if he was perceptive enough, he may figure that out. She needed a redirect. "I mean, would make an amazing romance hero."

"But you said make." He reached for her laptop, but she pulled it to her chest. "Reaching for my laptop is like me reaching for your gun."

"Not the same thing at all." He laughed. "You ever see the movie "Full Metal Jacket?""

She shook her head. "No. Why?"

He leaned in. "There's this scene when Marine recruits parade around the barracks in their underwear with their weapons doing this chant of "This is my rifle, this is my gun, this is for fighting, this is for fun." They touch their crotches at gun and fun. So, when you say touching your laptop is like touching my gun, it's not, sweet-heart. Touching my gun is all about fun. You want to give it a try?"

She couldn't move. Her whole body was paralyzed like he'd hit her with Harry Potter's Petrificus Totalus spell.

"You, okay?" he asked

"It's hot."

He smiled one of those you've-been-caught-smiles. And the only way out would be to confess or distract.

"Kiss me."

"Giving it a try then. I like that idea."

In a move quicker than Flame had cleared off the desk. Reese was in Brandon's lap, and she felt how at the ready his weapon was. The problem was that she wasn't sure how ready she was to go to war with this man. Not war really, but that's how her poetic brain worked. It put things into nice pretty little sentences that looked good on paper.

"Umm, I'm not sure I'd like to take that gun out for all the fun. I mean ... if we go to the range, do we have to shoot live rounds, or can we maybe see how it feels in my hand?" She groaned because that's not what she meant either. "Oh lord. That's not right. For a woman who deals with words, I sure don't have any when I need them."

"Reese. Just kiss me. My gun is happy and holstered."

She leaned into him and kissed him the way she would have if she were Pertussis on that desk. Her kisses were filled with wild abandon. She was that pirate, wearing the shamelessly low-cut blouse. She stripped him of his shirt and explored the ridges and valleys of muscles that she vowed to pen a letter and thank the United States Army for creating with their finely tuned exercise regimen.

She found herself rocking against his gun and realized it was all too much fun and far too public.

He picked her up, cupping her bottom while she gripped his neck. They were moving and shifting, and she didn't care where he took her. All she knew was she didn't want it to end and then it did. One minute she was Reese Arden in the arms of Brandon Fearless, and the next, she was Pertussis Loving being tossed overboard and drowning in the ocean. Her ship had sunk.

The cold water covered her head, and she sank to the bottom. She gulped in the water and opened her eyes only to see the murky depths. A tiny fish passed by and stopped to inspect her and then swam off as if disinterested.

She should have panicked, but she didn't. Instead, she sat at the bottom and realized she must have died.

Yes, that was it. She must have passed on. Kissing Brandon had been pure bliss; so perfect that her heart had given out. But why had she been tossed into this murky hell?

Then she realized she wasn't in hell at all. She was in the lake and her lungs hurt from holding her breath, and her arm ached from someone tugging at it. She pushed off the bottom and came out like a humpback breaching the water. She sucked in a huge breath and landed on her feet.

Standing waist deep next to her was Brandon with a big grin on his face.

"I was wondering when you were going to join me."

"You tossed me in the lake."

He nodded. "I did."

"W-w-why w-w-would you d-d-do that? I-I-I c-c-can't swim."

He moved toward her, and she clung to him, wrapping her jean-clad legs around his waist.

"Look at me."

He gripped her bottom and held her close to his body. His heat seeped through her wet clothes to warm her

"I've got you. Do you think I would have let you drown?"

"I thought we were ... you know."

"Oh, that is exactly where that was going, but I'd kind of like to approach it the old-fashioned way with dinner and flowers."

"You're old-fashioned?"

He brushed a kiss against her lips. "Weird, huh? I just can't help myself."

"Who would have thought?" She held on to him as if letting him go would send him to the depths forever.

"I've always had this old-school thing. Kind of a Doris Day or beyond vibe."

"Are you teasing me about my soundtrack?" She'd almost forgotten her Motown sounds blasting the day they'd met.

"Not at all. I've got my own classic vibe going when it comes to teenage crushes."

"I don't believe you. Who was your teenage crush?"

He moved her around the water, and she let go of her death grip on him.

Without missing a beat, he blurted, "Belle from *Beauty and the Beast*."

"Really?"

"What can I say? I like smart girls. I also like Claire from *Sixteen Candles*."

"Classic movie watcher? You're full of surprises." She kicked her feet and let herself float away from his body without letting go of his shoulders. "Why, because she was smart and pretty?"

He laughed. "Hell no. Because she could put her lipstick on with it tucked into her bra."

The laugh rolled through her like a tsunami, and she lost her grip on him, but something kicked in, and she paddled and kicked, and made it back to him safely.

"Look. I'm swimming. Brandon. I'm swimming."

He smiled in such a loving way that not even the cold water could keep the warmth from spreading through her.

"I know."

"You knew I could. How did you know?" She gasped. "You threw me in here on purpose."

He nodded. "The timing sucked, but neither of us were ready for what was about to happen."

She shook her head. "I was ready. The Pertussis inside me had already kicked off her boots and pushed aside her petticoats."

He lifted his brows. "I don't recall her wearing petticoats in what I'd read."

She opened her mouth and gasped. "Oh. My. Gosh. You read my manuscript."

He smiled. "I'm an early riser and I skimmed your notes. I liked him better as Brandon."

If she hadn't already died once that day in the murky depths of the lake and met indifference by the locals that swam beneath, she might have tried it again.

"I can't believe it."

"You're really good."

Some of the embarrassment eased away as his compliment washed over her.

"You think so?"

"I don't know much about love or love stories, but I'm enjoying Flame's and Pertussis' love story."

"Awful names," she said.

"Totally agree." He pulled her to him and kissed her until she forgot all about her silly characters and the book she was writing. "How did you know I could swim?"

"Doc told me. He has some stories about you."

"He does?"

He moved the hair behind her ear and rubbed his thumb over the scar. "He stitched this scar into place."

"I got that when I hit the bed frame."

He shook his head. "You got that taking a header off Bent-over-Betty."

She rubbed the small, raised scar. "My mom is such a liar."

"Maybe she was saving you from having to relive the trauma."

"More like saving herself."

She snuggled in closer to him. "Why do you think he acted like he didn't know me?"

He shrugged. "Maybe he was waiting for you to remember him. Honestly, I think Doc is the kind of guy that lets a story unfold when the time is right."

"I get it. Don't rush the ending." She smiled. "Is that why you dunked me in the lake?"

"That was self-preservation."

She risked a quick glance. "How is your gun now?" She kissed him softly.

"Behaving for now, but how about date night Tuesday. I hear there's a nice steak house called Trevi's in Copper Creek."

"A steakhouse? That sounds kind of fancy, and all I have is jeans."

He did that biting his lip thing and her whole body tingled. "I don't care what you're wearing. You could dress in a burlap bag and your fuzzy slippers, and I think you'd look sexy."

"I might try it just to see if you'd change your mind."

"I won't." He kissed her once more before he moved them toward the shore. "You're pruning, and I don't want you to use whooping cough as an excuse for getting out of our date."

"Is that a jab at my character?"

He rolled his eyes. "She dates a guy named flame."

Reese laughed. "True. So, it's a date."

"That it is."

CHAPTER TWENTY

He'd asked her on a date and had no car. Walking into Sheriff Cooper's office made him feel like a kid going to ask his dad for permission to borrow the station wagon, only he didn't have a dad.

If he was doing the dad thing, he should have gone to talk to Doc, but that felt more like a grandfather talk than a dad kind of thing. Aiden had that big brother vibe going, and Brandon liked him from the beginning.

He entered the office and looked around. There were several desks. Not one was bigger than the rest, and he liked that. There were no egos in this building. No one officer counted more than the next, or at least not in the head officer's eyes.

The ones who worked for him might see things differently, but from where Sheriff Cooper sat to the right, his position was the same as his deputies and his secretary who looked up from her computer.

"Oh, hey Brandon. What can we help you with?"

He felt like a kid in trouble because being in trouble was the only time he'd spent in a police station.

"I think he's here to see me," Aiden said. "Is that right?"

Brandon let out a sigh. "Yep."

The legs of his chair scraped against the linoleum flooring as the sheriff moved his chair back. "I was thinking about getting some lunch. You want to join me?"

"I'd love to."

Sheriff Cooper stopped at the desk that had a nameplate that read, Mark Bancroft. "This is Mark," and he pointed to the woman at the other desk, "That's his wife, Poppy." He nodded to the empty desk. "That's Merrick's place, but as I said, he'll be gone a bit now that his baby arrived."

"Congrats. What did he have?"

Poppy grinned, "A little girl named Aidy. Well, not so little. She weighed nearly nine pounds but then look at Merrick. There was no way that baby was going to be tiny."

Aiden tapped Mark's desk. "Hold down the fort, and don't let Mrs. Brown have you crawling up her tree after that new cat." He frowned. "What's this one's name?"

"Clyde," Mark said. "She already called twice. Said he was wearing a sombrero and boots."

Aiden turned to Brandon. "I'm telling you. There's never a dull day."

They walked out the door and down the block. About halfway, they crossed the street to the diner.

"This Mrs. Brown with the sombrero-wearing cat, does she have a granddaughter named Bailey?"

He whipped the diner door open, and the smell of fries hit Brandon like a sledgehammer to his carb-loving brain.

"Nope, just a common name. Mrs. Brown was married to Mr. Brown until he passed. I'm told it's because she dressed him in matching outfits with the old tomcat who took off last year. She picked up a new cat at the pound in Copper Creek, and I swear those poor cats do their best to escape, but she literally holds them hostage by their costumes. If Clyde is in a sombrero and boots, he's probably been lassoed to something as well."

"Poor cat."

Aiden pointed to the booth by the window. "I take this one. It gives me a glimpse into my world."

Maisey walked by with her swinging coffee pot. "Marina said she wanted you to bring her a BLT on rye when you leave."

Aiden laughed. "You see, there are no secrets in this town."

Maisey overturned the mugs and poured them both a cup. "I figured you both need to be fully loaded since you've got the night shift with Merrick gone." She turned to Brandon. "And you've got a date."

He stared at her with his mouth hanging half-open. "What else do you know?"

"You need a car."

She pulled her keys from her pocket and set them on the table. "My wagon is in the back. It's had its fair share of knockin' boots in the back. It ain't pretty to look at, but it runs fine." She went to turn around. "My Raquel Welch wig is back there. I hear you've taken a fancy to it, but you leave it alone. That wig cost me nearly sixty bucks on QVC. I'll have your blue-plate specials up in a moment." She was gone in a second.

"Did we order blue plate specials?" Brandon asked.

"There are times when you pick and choose your battles. What you're eating at Maisey's isn't one of them." Aiden's phone chimed, and he chuckled. "You don't argue with my wife either. Turns out you've got a four o'clock hair appointment at Cove Cuts. She said don't be late because she's got an appointment with a pretty girl named Reese right after you, and she doesn't want to keep her waiting."

"You guys are something else."

"We're something all right."

A few minutes later, Maisey dropped off something that looked like Salisbury steak. He couldn't be certain, but it was some type of patty drowned in mushroom gravy served with cheesy mashed potatoes and peas.

"What do you want to be when you grow up?" Aiden asked.

That was an interesting question, and one he'd never been asked.

"I'm just taking it one day at a time. Sometimes tomorrow seems too far away."

Aiden took a bite and seemed to savor the food or the thought for a long time. "It's coming one way or another."

"In my life, it's been like an overflowing river I can't seem to contain."

Aiden looked at him. "All you need are a few sandbags and a shovel. The best way to control the flow of your life is to redirect it when it seems to travel off the beaten path. While things are good, you shore up the foundation and secure it. That way when the storm comes, and the water rises, you're ready.

"Philosophically, that sounds amazing, but you and I both know the sky opens up, and the rain comes down when you least expect it."

Aiden laughed. "That's when you ask for help and hope your friends have gators and rowboats." He pulled his keys from his pocket and slid them across the table. "You can take my SUV. It was built within the last four years, has working taillights, and you don't have to pop the clutch to start it. Did you need anything else?"

"No, I was going to ask for the car." He hung his head. "Feels silly now. I mean, you don't even know me, but if I had a big brother, you'd be the kind of guy I would have liked him to be."

"I always wanted to be a big brother. And as your adopted big brother, if you put a single dent in my car, I'm going to kick your ass."

Brandon smiled. "Deal."

Maisey swung by and filled their cups. "What? You're not taking my love buggy to Copper Creek?"

Brandon settled his hand over hers. "I don't want to spoil her on the first date."

Maisey giggled. "Oh, you're a charmer. If my math is right, that will be sometime around spring."

"What's that, Maisey?" Aiden asked.

"The next birth in Aspen Cove."

"Oh, no," Brandon said. "It's just a date. Neither of us are residents. We have one foot in town and the other out."

Maisey smiled. "That's what you say now but mark my words. Someone is having a baby next spring."

"And you think it's me?"

Aiden laughed. "That would be something, wouldn't it?"

"Never happen. I'd make a terrible father. I came from a long line of them."

The door opened, and in walked Doc. Aiden waved him over. "Doc, join us."

Doc looked over his shoulder to his corner booth. "It will cost ya, and I ain't a cheap date." He lowered himself next to Brandon and shimmied himself over until Brandon was trapped between the old doctor and the window.

"What's the dilemma?"

"No dilemma," Brandon said.

Aiden leaned back and crossed his arms behind his head. "Sure, there is. We were talking about Brandon and Reese having their first child by spring of next year."

Doc's bushy brows shot straight up. "Son, you ain't even been on a date yet. My advice is to glove it before you love it. You don't buy the cow before you taste the milk."

"See." He pulled at the collar of this T-shirt, feeling it tighten with every passing second. "I haven't even been on a date with the girl, and you guys have me married with children."

Aiden smiled. "Not true. No one said anything about married, and Maisey only gave you one kid."

"As I said, I come from a long line of losers. I refuse to be another in a string of them."

Aiden slapped the table, causing the silverware to jump. "And that's where you come in Doc. Is parenthood a nature or a nurture thing? I mean, are you born a shitty parent, or can you do better when you know better?"

"Definitely a nature thing. I've never met a kid out of the womb ready to take on fatherhood. Hell, I've never met a father fully ready to take on fatherhood. You think you are until your sweet little angel flushes your dentures down the toilet. Right then, you turn into someone capable of murder."

Maisey stopped by with another blue plate special and a cup of coffee for Doc before her squeaky white shoes took her away.

"Let me tell you a story about my Phyllis. She was the sweetest thing ever until one Valentine's Day when Charlie was six."

Doc didn't get mashed potatoes like the rest of us. He got fries and mopped them across the gravy before gobbling up a few.

"As a country doctor, I'm not always paid in cash. We used to be pork rich but cash poor. We'd never starve, but my poor Phyllis never had the sofa she wanted nor the curtains she coveted from that Montgomery Ward Catalog. That damn book had more earmarks than our bible. It certainly got read more. Anyway, one day, I was working on the blue goose." He pointed out the window at the old 57 Chevy truck parked in front of the diner. "I've had that old girl all these years. Doctoring was a cash-rich crop that year, and I got my Phyllis those curtains she wanted. You know the one's with the embroidered watermelons on the edge?"

Brandon didn't have a clue, but he nodded because he could see them in his mind's eye. Brandon stared at Aiden, not knowing where this was going but afraid to say a word. The sheriff had that stay-with-me look to him, and he was pinned against the window, so he didn't have much choice. It was kind of like being stuck in a foxhole in enemy territory, except this one had Salisbury steak and decent coffee.

"I'm with you."

Doc cleared his throat. "You ever take the cap off a carburetor and strip the skin straight from your fingertips? Well, I did that day, and I told Charlie to run inside and get me a cloth from the table. Oh, she did all right. She got the new curtains I'd given to Phyllis for Valentine's Day. My lovely wife, who'd spent every second of her life loving on that little girl of ours from the day she was born, was the first exorcism I've ever experienced, and there was no priest present. Poor Charlie spent that night at Bea's because she was certain her mama was going to kill her, and I wasn't too sure she wouldn't either. The point is, we aren't born bad. We all have bad moments. Some of us have lots of them."

"What if I'm one of those that are on a perpetual bad cycle?"

"You're not."

"How can you say that? How would you know?"

"Because you have an empathy gene. When you do bad, you feel bad, right?"

He felt awful when he hurt someone. "I do."

"That's that built-in meter that makes you a good human."

"What about Phyllis?"

"She cried all night because she'd cared more about some watermelon curtains than she did in that one split second about her daughter. And the silly thing was when she cleaned the curtains; she hung them, but not because she liked them. She hated those curtains, but she hung them because they reminded her every day that nothing was sweeter than the love of her child."

"What am I supposed to take out of this conversation?"

Doc shrugged. "I don't care what you take out of it as long as you pay for my lunch." He picked up his coffee, took a swig, and turned to Brandon. "Condoms are on sale at the pharmacy, and I spoke to Katie. She said if you're staying in town, she can rent you the apartment above the bakery. Just stop by her house for the keys when you need them."

Doc picked up his plate. "Looks like my work is done here. You two enjoy your day." The older man took his plate to his corner booth, and Maisey brought Brandon the bill.

"What just happened?"

"You might have gotten the best advice you've ever received."

Brandon looked out the window. "What did he tell me?"

"That you're a good man, and a good person, and that you need to believe in yourself. Your intentions speak as loud as your actions."

"He said all that?"

Aiden laughed. "Yes, and condoms were on sale, and if you don't want to make Maisey right, I'd pick up a package before that date tonight."

CHAPTER TWENTY-ONE

The last few days were like playing house in a utopian world. She woke to coffee and the muffin of the day sitting on the table. She'd relax on the deck sipping coffee and enjoying her treat while watching a more delectable one take a morning swim. Nothing started a day better than a nearly naked man, an ideal setting, and breakfast.

Brandon Fearless cut through the water like a hot knife cut through butter. She didn't know what stroke he swam, but it was flawless each time his body breached the water reaching for air. Never in her life had the word sluice been so damn sexy than when he broke the surface, and she watched the water slide from his skin.

Just thinking about that mornings' sluicing made her feel dirty and in need of a shower. Or maybe it was thinking about their date that made her all hot and sweaty and in need of some sluicing herself.

Since their almost all the way moment, they hadn't done anything but hug and kiss, but oh those kisses were on the edge of so much more, and they gave a glimpse of what the potential of more could be. More was barbecue burgers at the end of the day. It was snuggles by the fire while she talked about books, and he talked about his favorite movies. It was water fights in the kitchen while listening to Gladys Knight and the Pips, and then discussing why they called themselves the Pips.

Today when she woke, on the table was her name neatly handwritten across the front of a lime green envelope. Inside was a note from Katie.

Reese,

You have a five o'clock hair appointment. Don't worry about what to wear. I've got you covered.

Katie

How could she have possibly known?

The rest of the afternoon was spent with her new best friend Pertussis Loving and her old best friend Z. One helped her live in a fantasy world while the other held her tethered to this one with his need for kibble and attention.

She ignored two calls from her mother and promised herself that she'd call back tomorrow. She knew if she let her into her life today, Mom would ruin the overall positive vibe that flowed through Reese.

Besides, there was so much that needed to be addressed. It hadn't escaped her attention that her mother had completely lied to her all these years.

It baffled the mind when she considered all the times she spent in therapy trying to figure out why she stuttered. Her mother's standard line was that she'd never experienced any type of trauma that could cause a kid that type of distress, but honesty wasn't really in her mother's wheelhouse. She still didn't know who her father was. For all Reese knew, he was the mailman or according to her mother a real live stork that delivered babies to veterinarians because they were too busy to have their own puppies.

The more she thought about her life the more frustrated she

became. What the hell happened all those years ago? She rubbed at the scar behind her ear that had started to ache. It was as if the mention of her mom made it red and angry. Maybe she was the one who should not be named. Would her mother be her Voldemort?

"What the hell, mom? I nearly drowned?" Things were different since her writer's brain had taken a magical mystery tour since the big reveal. As far as Reese knew, some mythical creature pulled her from the depths of the lake at Aspen Cove and laid her on the shore. Hell, it could have been the minnow she saw the other day. Maybe that's why it stopped and stared at her for a second. It was probably looking at her saying, "Oh, you again. I thought I squared you away decades ago."

She glanced at the clock and her heart took off like Z did when he chased a bird down the beach. She had a date tonight, and the town was coming together to make sure they turned this duckling into a swan.

With her keys in her hand, she and Z climbed into her car and drove into town listening to the song that started it all, "Stop in the Name of Love"

A smile took over her face. Brandon Fearless was exactly the kind of man she could love. He was selfless and centered. He was a soldier who sacrificed himself to save others. Everything he'd done in his life had been done for the betterment of someone else. She'd never known anyone who'd put service before self.

She pulled into the only spot open in front of Cove Cuts and debated on taking Z inside with her. When he jumped out, the decision was made.

"Okay, you get to come now, but you have to stay home tonight. No dogs on the date."

Z didn't seem to care because animals lived in the moment. There was something to be learned from them. They didn't hold grudges. They didn't worry about their next meal or whether they had a great outfit for their date. They didn't care if their fur was curled, or their fangs were brushed. They were there right then, and that's what you got.

She opened the door and was greeted by a beautiful brunette.

"Come inside." The woman smiled sunshine and rainbows. "I'm Marina." She whipped a cape off the back of the chair. "I love your curls."

Reese was always self-conscious about her curly hair and its red hue. She imagined she got both from her father since her mother had neither.

"I've never been a fan."

"Seriously?"

"I suppose that's the way of it. You always want what you don't have."

Marina smiled. "Oh, back in the day, my wants were pretty simple, and they had nothing to do with my hair."

Reese had heard Marina's story and felt a sense of shame for being so shallow to think having curls was a major life crisis.

"The town talks and I heard your story. I can't imagine."

"No one can until it becomes their story, but every person has a story, and no story is better or worse, they are simply different. This date is part of your story. Maybe it's a little part or maybe it's the beginning of everything. Here's the question. Do you want your forever to begin with curly hair or straight hair?"

She tapped her chin. That was a good question. Being authentic was always important. Brandon seemed to like her for her, and if she changed things too much would he like her less? Did changing the outside do something to the inside? She'd seen women get a complete makeover, and one would think nothing would happen to their personality, but it did. It was like the outside transformation created an internal vortex and sucked out all the goodness. It was as if a sweetness enema had removed all the sugar from their insides.

"Keep the curls. They're part of who I am."

"I'm glad to hear it."

The door opened and in walked Katie with two pink boxes cradled in her arms. "I brought clothes and cookies." She opened the clothing box first which contained two dresses—one pink and one yellow. Then she opened the cookie box. "I've got a plan. If the clothes don't fit, then we force-feed you the cookies until the dresses fit perfectly." She pulled out a yellow sundress. "I love this one, and think it says, 'I'm sweet, but if you buy the good wine I might put out.'" She giggled and draped it over a nearby chair.

She took out the pink dress with the tiny little bows covering the buttons. "This one says I want you to be my daddy." She winked. "Or as Bowie might say, it says, 'you've been a bad girl and need a spankin'.'"

"Oh, my goodness. Are you serious?"

Katie laughed and shook her head, "No, but I love that you thought I was. Both are very sweet and say whatever you want. I've got the perfect pair of cowboy boots for each if you wear anything between a seven and an eight and a half." She waved her hand in the air. "I went through several sizes during my pregnancy."

"Why are you guys doing this?"

Marina smiled. "Because our daughters are years from dating."

Katie laughed. "Oh, puhlease, you know our daughters are never dating. Our husbands will never allow it. I'm doing it because I'm a sucker for love. I never thought it was a possibility in my life, and now I want to see it be a reality in everyone's."

Marina ran her hands through Reese's hair. "What she said. There is nothing as beautiful as love."

"This isn't love. It's a date."

Both women smiled at each other.

"It's got to start somewhere."

A half an hour later, Reese left feeling like Ally Sheedy from

The Breakfast Club. She'd never considered herself a beauty but an outlier. She was a single pea in a pile of carrots. A shell in a jar of sand. Leaving Cove Cuts in a yellow sundress, cowboy boots, and her hair tied back in a ribbon made her feel different. She walked to her car feeling taller and prouder and prettier.

When she got back to the house, she opened a bottle of wine and sat on the deck waiting for her date to arrive. What if he stood her up?

CHAPTER TWENTY-TWO

What if she wasn't there when he arrived? He looked at the flowers on the seat of the SUV. Were three dozen too many? He couldn't decide between the roses, the daisies, and the mixed bouquet. A wise man might have gone with the bouquet and been done with it, but they didn't have that yellow rose dipped in sunshine in it, and it was special. It wasn't quite yellow or red but a blend of both. The florist told him it was called Miracle. He figured it was a sign because she said yes to the date and that was miracle enough for him.

He had to believe she'd be there when he got to the front door. In truth, he knew she was because her car was in the driveway.

He gathered the flowers and walked toward the door. He had a smart new haircut and the brand-new outfit Marina handed him when he walked out the door. He had no idea how she knew his size, but she'd sized him up pretty good. She told him he could use the khaki pants if he decided to come on board with the sheriff's department. He imagined she'd pilfered them from her husband's uniform storage closet. As for the shirt ... that was probably from Aiden's personal closet, and he promised to return it after it was laundered.

His heart's pace picked up as he approached the home he'd been living in all week. What was laid back and relaxed yesterday felt different tonight. Like somehow, the girl he'd been kissing all week had changed, and he didn't have a right to take her out.

He stood on the porch pacing and force-feeding himself doubt. She was a college-educated woman who should have known better than to date a man like him. He had little to offer her. It wasn't that he was stupid. He was far from it. He'd proven time and again that he could do anything he applied himself to. The problem was that life didn't give him many opportunities in which to apply himself.

He let out a growl. It was time to stop the negative talk and get on with the night because this was most likely all he'd get with Reese. Their paths had crossed for now, but their futures were uncertain.

Though the idea of staying in Aspen Cove had its merits, he'd never been able to plant seeds and grow anywhere. The concept was foreign.

Standing on the mat that said welcome, he held the three groups of flowers and pressed the doorbell.

Z's loud woof was followed by the *click clack* of shoes. The door opened and he was convinced the sun shone from inside of the house to outside. Reese stood there in a yellow dress and cowboy boots looking like a ray of perfection.

"Wow, just wow."

She looked at the flowers.

"Wow, just wow. Did you rob a florist?"

He glanced at all the blooms which seemed both excessive and not close to being enough.

"If I did, I didn't steal enough of them." He took her in once more. "You look amazing."

Her smile lit up her entire being.

Z danced around them, and Brandon used his free hand to ruffle his fur.

"You look good too, buddy." He held out the flowers to Reese. "These are for you. Should we put them in water before we go?"

"Yes." She led them into the kitchen where they worked side-by-side to cut the stems and arrange the flowers into some old vases they found under the kitchen sink.

On their way out, he stopped her at the front door. "If I forget to tell you." He cupped her face and looked deep into her eyes. "This is the best date I've ever had, and we haven't even gotten to the good stuff."

She giggled. "What's the good stuff."

He brushed his lips against hers. "Dessert and the goodnight kiss." He placed his hand at the small of her back and guided her to Aiden's SUV.

"Where did you get the car?"

He opened her door and then pointed to his pants and shirt. "Same place I got my outfit. I borrowed them." He let out a slow whistle. "This town is really something."

He closed the door and rounded the front before taking his place behind the steering wheel.

"Are you ready?"

She wiggled in her seat. "I am. It's been a very long time since I've been on a date."

He shook his head as he backed out of the driveway.

"What's wrong with men?"

She laughed.

"They tend to value their hearing."

He reached over and took her hand. "It's never been a problem for me."

She squeezed his palm. "Why is that?"

"Life has taught me over and over again that it's short, and if you don't pay attention, you might miss something. It doesn't much matter if the person repeats it a dozen times or not. What needs to be said, needs to be said. If someone is speaking, then give them the courtesy of a listen."

She groaned. "Unless you're my mother. I've ignored her messages all week."

"You've got history. That's different. Once you've established a pattern, you can make an informed decision."

"What was your last date?" she asked.

"Two MRE meals and a flare in a canyon in Afghanistan."

"Oooh, sounds romantic."

He smiled. "Hey, as far as desert warfare goes, it wasn't bad."

"How did it end?"

"That's where it went bad. She was a selfish date. She refused to share her brownie."

"You wanted her to share her brownie?" She let her jaw drop in mock horror.

He knew she was yanking his chain by the way she over-dramatized her reaction.

"What about you?"

"There weren't any MRE's or selfish dessert moments." She turned in her seat and tugged at her seat belt but never let go of his hand, and he liked that. She was holding on to him and keeping him in a way that no one ever had.

"I can't say I've truly been on a real date. Things just kind of happened. Girls like me weren't the ones you went after. We were the ones you ended up with when no one else was left."

That statement made his insides burn with white-hot fire he had to tamp down.

"Well, Ms. Arden, tonight, you're here because I want you in the worst way. You are not the booby prize, but the first prize. If we were at the county fair, you'd be that big bear hanging on the hook in the arcade. You know the one ... that pretty pink or white bear that every girl wants their boyfriend to win. The one that no one ever does because it's out of reach. It's so damn special and cost a lot of tickets." He watched the blush reach her cheeks and he knew he'd made his point. "You are worth more than that bear."

Up ahead was the sign for Trevi's Steakhouse and he pulled into the front so the valet could park the car.

They entered the restaurant and various smells bounced around them. He was trained to pay attention to his surroundings and right now they were covered in a cloak of butter and char-grilled goodness.

The host led them to a table next to a window that overlooked a canyon where the setting sun made the orange-colored rocks appear on fire.

Dinner was amazing from the wedge salad to the double fudge brownie they shared for dessert. The time flew by and before he knew it, they were pulling in front of the lake house. Only this time, the driveway was full.

"Oh my God. I cannot believe it."

Reese didn't wait for him. She threw her door open and stomped up the stairs and into the house. He ran after her.

"Mother," she yelled. "Where are you?"

"Stop your screaming," a voice came from the deck. "What will the neighbors think?"

"Y-y-you d-d-don't b-b-belong here."

A woman with brown hair and darker eyes entered the house and set her wineglass on the counter. Brandon took in Reese's mom and couldn't see the resemblance at all. Before him stood a woman who looked more like the Malamute than she did her daughter.

"Hi," he said moving forward and offering his hand. "I'm—"

"I don't care who you are. You're irrelevant. You know it. I know it. The problem is ..." she shook her head. "In her naivety, she doesn't."

"Mother."

Her mother rolled her eyes and put her hands on her hips. "It's true. You're not his forever. You're his tonight girl." She turned to Brandon. "Am I right?" She narrowed her eyes. "You got a ring in that pocket and soliloquies of love ready for the proposal?"

He wasn't ready to walk down the aisle, but this wasn't what she was making it out to be.

"Don't disrespect your daughter."

"Me?" She laughed. "I wasn't the one who calculated what three dozen flowers and a nice dinner would get."

"Mother. Get out." Reese pointed to the door.

Her mom went to the open wine bottle and poured herself another glass. "Don't forget who owns this house."

Reese stomped her foot.

"He's a paying guest."

Her mother laughed. "No, he's not. He's staying here as a favor, and you're not part of the bargain. Really, Reese, you need to hold yourself to a higher standard."

Brandon had been in the crosshairs of enemy fire that felt less brutal.

"You're not being fair to your daughter."

"Me? What about you? What were you going to do? Love her tonight and leave her next week? I've lived that scenario, and I want more for her." Her mother tossed back the wine and poured herself another glass. "It's time for you to leave. It will be easier on everyone."

He knew her mother was right. They had no forever plan. They were like dry tinder and playing with matches. When their fire ignited, as it would have when they got home, it would have burned hot. Someone was bound to get burned. This was a blessing in disguise, really.

He turned and walked to his room where he tossed his things in his rucksack.

"You're letting her win?"

He shook his head.

"No, I'm making sure you don't lose. Don't you understand? She's right. I've got nothing to offer you." He moved down the hallway to the front door.

"You could have offered me something no one ever had—your heart."

CHAPTER TWENTY-THREE

A lump the size of Colorado stuck in her throat and tears as big as Aspen Cove Lake ran down her cheeks. She wanted to rail at the world but the person on her radar right now was her mother. She moved like a category five storm into the kitchen.

"What is wrong with you?" Reese yelled. "You just ruined the best night of my life."

Her mother leaned against the counter and sipped her wine.

"I just saved you from making the worst mistake of your life."

"How do you know I haven't been making that mistake since the day I told you I laid him out flat on the deck and had my way with him?"

Her mom snorted. "Because I know you and I taught you better. If there was one lesson I pounded into your brain, that was don't make the same mistake I made."

"Jeez, Mom. You make it sound like I was the worst thing that ever happened to you."

Her mother sighed. "You know that's not true but raising you on my own wasn't easy. As far as you 'doing him on the deck,' I know you."

"Oh no, you don't. You think you know me, but you only know what you want to know." She picked up the bottle of wine with the Prosecco label. "Take this, for instance. I hate it. I like a wine that makes my lips pucker. Give me a good cab any day. If it makes my eyes cross, then even better."

"You love this wine." Her mother pulled a glass from the cupboard and filled it to the top handing it to Reese. "Drink up."

Reese stared at the glass before picking it up and throwing it across the room. She cleared the furniture in the living room and hit the stone fireplace. The wine bled into the rock and surrounding mortar. "I only drink it because you like it. I'm a pleaser. Or I used to be but, no more."

Her mother gasped. "Why would you do that? Look at the mess you made?" She picked up the roll of paper towels and rushed into the living room.

"Leave it," Reese screamed

"But it's a bloody mess."

"Yes, it's a mess, but you make a mess of everything and never notice. Did you hear a single word I said? I hate the damn wine."

"Fine, did you have to throw it across the room?"

"Yes, because you didn't listen to me." She tossed her hands in the air. "You never listen."

Her mother stomped her foot. "I always listen. You're like a record on repeat."

Reese took a few calming breaths because if she didn't, there was a very good chance the wine would turn into a real bloody mess. For a split second, she wondered if there had ever been a murder in Aspen Cove or if her mother's would be the first.

"Who broke you?"

"No one broke me. What are you talking about?"

"You're so wounded that you spend your life hurting others, so they hurt worse than you? You're one of those who kill people one nick at a time, but they never truly understand that they're bleeding to death because they are dying by a thousand tiny cuts."

"You're crazy."

"That's my point, Mom. You can't, even for a second, think about what I said, or notice that I've been speaking clearly and concisely since I got home."

Her mother stopped for a second and cocked her head to the side in the same way Z did when he wasn't quite sure what he heard or when he was processing the words to make sure they didn't have the word 'treat' in them.

"Not true. You yammered on when you first arrived."

Reese made a checkmark on her virtual scorecard in the sky. Her reference to yammering was a razor-sharp cut to put Reese in her place.

"I'll keep score for you because it's so important to keep me down. In fact, let's just call the game mom because I'm not playing any more. You win all the games, but in the process, you lose me."

"What do you mean I lose you. I can't lose you, I'm your mother."

"That's a card you've played far too often, along with the 'you need me game' that you play, but that's not true. I don't need you. It's you who needs me."

Her mother's gaze dropped to her shoes. "Where did you get those ridiculous boots?"

Reese screamed and stomped in place. "Pay attention. You may learn something." She grabbed the paper towels and sopped up the wine that puddled on the floor. Then she swept up the glass with a wad of towels because she didn't want Z getting his paws cut.

"I don't know what you're getting at."

Reese shook her head. "You wouldn't because you are so self-involved. Did you know that when a parent has a child, they're actually supposed to be the one who does the raising? You kept me under your thumb, not because I couldn't do without you but because you couldn't do without me. I was under the impression that I was the one who failed to launch, but it was you wasn't it?"

"That's not true."

"Sixteen and knocked up. All these years and I was so proud of you because of who you became. You were a mother and a veterinarian and you owned half of this amazing house." She twirled in a circle. "It is an amazing house." She walked to the deck. "Why didn't we ever visit? I have a single memory of coming here when I was five years old. It's of me and Uncle Frank playing chess." She smiled. "I am a proficient cheat. You know what else I'm good at?" She pointed to the shadow of Bent-over-Betty. "I'm an excellent swimmer, but you knew that. I bet I'm not nearly as good of a swimmer as you are a liar."

"How dare you?" Her mother said.

"Me? You allowed me to go to therapy and believe I'd never had a lick of trauma in my life when I'd nearly drowned in that lake."

"No one knows what happened."

"Brandy knew what happened. She was there," Reese said.

"She was an unreliable witness."

"Why was I with a ten-year-old? Where were you?"

"I'm not on trial here."

"Should you be? You were a twenty-something mom with a five-year-old who nearly drowned. Where were you?"

"I was down the beach. I saw your father, and I went to talk to him."Her mother buried her head. "Worst day of my life. There's just so much to tell."

Reese took a seat. "You chased my date away. I've got nothing else to do. I'd say you owe me some answers. Let's start with my father."

Her mother shook her head. "He never knew about you."

"Ever, as in you never told him you were pregnant?"

Her mother sank into a chair on the deck. "No. Grandma threatened me within an inch of my life. Your father was working class."

"We're working class."

Her mother laughed. "Oh honey, the Arden's aren't working class, I just choose to work, and I chose to make you work, but you never had to."

"Wait. I'm rich?"

Her mother laughed. "No, I'm rich, and Frank is rich. The last time I checked, you were a starving artist."

Reese always knew her grandmother held her birth against her. Grandma was the original mean girl and made Ursula look like a friendly mermaid. She wanted to be furious at her mother but weren't we all a product of our upbringing? Her mother was lucky she didn't find herself shipped off to a convent. Reese wasn't sure if it was luck or not, but it was a surprise that she wasn't put up for adoption or that her mother wasn't shipped off to some aunt in Sheboygan, Wisconsin. The only reason she wasn't was because there was no aunt in Wisconsin. "That day when I nearly drowned, where were you?"

"That day you were with Brandy, and I turned my back for what seemed like a minute, and I followed him down the beach. I should have known he would have moved on." Reese had never seen her mother's face look so sad. "It had been five years, and he already had more blooms started in another vase of flowers." It was an odd way to describe a family, but her mother was an oddball, to say the least. "I didn't have the heart to disrupt the life they'd begun. I'd already been unfair to him, and you, and to me by keeping you a secret. It's something I'll regret forever, but not something I could change. You don't get to go back."

"So, my father is a local." She let her mind race to place every face she'd seen since her arrival, but none screamed daddy.

"I'm surprised the town hasn't coughed up that secret too," her mother said.

It became apparent that Aspen Cove held many more mysteries that it hadn't divulged about the Arden's. "Why didn't you tell me I'd drowned. Why did you keep that secret?"

Her mother buried her face in her hands, and she cried. "Because my mother told me I'd failed as a parent, and she was right. I'd failed. I'd let my guard down twice for that boy, and I was ashamed. The one thing that I promised you when I had you was that I would be the best parent ever, and I wasn't. I nearly allowed you to die. You better believe that from that day on I was on you like lint on tape. When you didn't remember that day ... I wasn't going to remind you what a terrible parent you had." The tears ran down mom's cheeks in torrents. She seemed to wilt and it broke Reese's heart.

"You were a lot more fun before I was five."

Her mother sniffled. "I agree. I love you, Reese, but you haven't been easy to parent."

"I love you too, Mom, but you haven't been easy either." She rose and walked toward the hallway.

"Where are you going?"

"I'm not really sure. But right now, I'm going to bed. Tomorrow is a new chapter in a new book of my life. I'd suggest you start a new chapter on yours. I can't be responsible for writing your happy ending, Mom. I love you, and I know you love me too. We just need to love ourselves better."

"What are you going to do about that boy? You know honey, you can do better."

Reese stopped and turned to face her mother. "That boy is a man, and the truth is I'm probably not worth his time." The honesty of that statement made her stomach hurt. "You know what he has that we don't? He's got a sense of self. And he's got integrity. While I'd love to run after him, it's not the right thing to do right now because I'd do anything to get him to take me back, and I'm not sure that would be wise for either of us. He needs to be needed, but he needs to know that I need him for the right reasons. It's because I love and care about him. That poor man has been rescuing people his whole life. He's got a savior complex, and I don't want to be the next in a long line of people who take from him. I want to be someone who gives him what he needs. Maybe it's time someone else did the rescuing."

"Oh Reese, I know you love your books, but there is no white knight."

Reese walked back to her mother and kissed her cheek. "You really need to read more, Mom."

CHAPTER TWENTY-FOUR

Brandon dropped off the keys to Aiden and changed his clothes at the station. He told the sheriff how much he appreciated the loan of the car, and that he'd consider the offer of the job even though he knew he wouldn't. Once he drowned his sorrows in his beer, he'd be getting on the road, and he meant that in the most literal sense— boots to the pavement.

Bishop's Brewhouse was empty, but it was Tuesday, so he didn't expect a big crowd. As he moved inside, there were the usual suspects, Mike the cat sat on the old register swishing the keys with his tail, a group of guys sat by the window with a pitcher of beer, and a rougher looking crowd gathered around the pool table. Among them was Dalton who smiled proudly each time one of his friends slapped his back and congratulated him on the birth of baby Ransom.

At the bar was Doc who patted the stool beside him.

"I was wondering when you were going to pay off that debt you owed me." He rubbed at the bushy mustache that sat like a wild animal below his nose. "I didn't think you'd be doing it on date night." Doc frowned. "If you already went through the whole box you bought, you and I need to talk about enjoying the moment."

"It's not that Doc. The box is full."

Though Brandon hadn't officially met Cannon, he recognized the man when he walked out of the back room.

"Hey, Brandon." He gave him a strange look. "Wait. Don't you have a date?"

"You too? Is my life on speed dial in this town?"

Cannon dried his hands off on a nearby towel and offered him one to shake. "There are no secrets. Who needs security cameras when we got wives and mothers? I'm Cannon by the way, and your neighbor. Sorry about the last-minute cancellation, but you wouldn't have wanted what we got. It wasn't pretty. Came out of both ends of the baby for days."

"Nice to meet you, and it worked out okay for a bit."

"A bit?" Cannon asked.

Doc picked up his beer and took a drink, leaving some bubbles on his mustache. "Obviously, lover boy has gotten himself into some trouble or he wouldn't be sitting here on date night." He turned to face Brandon. "What the hell did you do boy?"

Cannon laughed. "Oh, I feel a lecture coming on, and when they start, I disappear." He pointed to the taps. "You know where the beer is, and you know where I'll be. You two have fun." Cannon pointed to the guys at the pool table. "Make sure they don't drink me out of a business." He disappeared as fast as he came.

"You want to start from the beginning or get straight to the point?"

Brandon rose and went behind the bar and pulled himself a beer. It seemed like tonight was going to be self-serve all the way around. He reached for Doc's beer and topped it off.

"The date-night part was amazing. Reese looked perfect. The restaurant was amazing, and the food was great. That steak was almost as good as I get in Texas. If I didn't know better, I would have said they sliced it straight from the ass of that cow right before they grilled it. It was that fresh and delicious." He slid the beers into place and rounded the bar before taking his spot next to Doc again. "Did you know they went to Arizona and cut their own mesquite wood? That's how they get that deep smokey taste."

Doc's eyes narrowed. "Are you going to Bobby Flay me into a coma or are you going to tell me what in the hell happened tonight?"

Brandon chuckled. Of all the people he'd miss in town, he'd miss Doc. The old man might have been curmudgeonly, but he was exactly who Brandon would have pictured if he'd had a grandfather.

"Her mother happened."

Doc picked up his beer and gulped. "In my experience, mothers are generally the easy ones. It's the daddies you have to win over. They're the ones with shotguns and bad attitudes."

"Reese doesn't have a dad."

Doc laughed. "Oh son, no wonder you have a box of unused condoms." He laughed so hard, the rough looking dudes at the pool table stopped what they were doing just to see what the fuss was about. "I'm going to need to give you a lesson in biology. You see there's this thing called a penis and—"

"Geez Doc, I know how to use my junk. That wasn't the problem. I just ... got a wake-up call. Her mom was standing there asking me if I had a ring in my pocket, and if I had pretty words picked out for the proposal."

Again, Doc busted out in a belly laugh. "Killed the mood, huh? Well, I imagine that was the intent. I don't know much about Sara. She didn't come around much since she was a teen and got caught hiding the worm herself. As far as Reese not having a daddy ..." Doc whistled. "Look around son, there's a face just like hers out there. It ain't as pretty, but it's here."

"You think she was just trying to scare me away?" He felt like a fool.

"I don't know the woman. All I know is Reese is old enough to make up her mind. It would be a shame if you made it up for her. Seems to me as if she just got her voice back, let her use it."

Her voice came in loud and clear as he left tonight. What was it that she said to him? She told him he could have offered her his heart. Little did she know that she already had it.

"I'm a stupid asshole."

Doc finished his beer and set it on the bar.

"We can't help ourselves." He pulled out his phone and dialed a number. "Brandon needs the keys to the apartment." There was some mumbling and then Doc grunted. "I'll tell him." He hung up and slid off the stool. "I've had two beers, and I'm a good tipper. You go get that girl of yours and ask her to forgive you. You're a stupid fool, and she knows it, but Reese is a romantic and will give you a second chance. You two are looking for the same thing, and it doesn't come along that often." He took a step toward the door. "Keys to the apartment above the bakery are under the mat in the alleyway." He shuffled toward the door and stopped and then turned and walked back. "I almost forgot." He took a seat again and took on a serious expression. "I called in that favor. Your sister was not using. She was clean."

It was like a thousand-pound weight lifted from his chest. He wanted to laugh and cry at the same time.

"But it said toxicity."

"The liver failed."

That was exactly what Reese said. "I just don't understand any of it. Nothing makes sense."

Doc set his hand on his shoulder. "It rarely does."

"I spent my life trying to save her and for what?"

Doc smiled. "Maybe it all came to this moment."

"What do you mean?"

Doc shook his head. "I don't try to understand the meaning of life. I just live it. You were born, and you exist. Certain events bring you to certain places. Do they mean something? Only you know. X marks the spot, son." Doc turned and left again.

Brandon took two twenties from his wallet and set them on the counter. He called to the back to let Cannon know the counter was unmanned before walking across the street to the alleyway behind the bakery, and just like Doc said, the key was under the mat.

He walked up the stairway and entered the apartment that smelled like brown sugar and cinnamon. The only thing it was missing was his heart.

He dropped his rucksack and headed back out. He had everything to lose if he walked away tonight and nothing to gain if he left Aspen Cove without telling Reese what she meant to him. He'd never felt home until she opened the door and let him in.

The closer he got to Lake Circle, the faster his pace became. His mind raced with how it would play out. Would he be the gentleman and knock on the door or would he black ops the hell out of it and take her hostage. He didn't have to do either because right under Bent-over-Betty exactly where the pink letter had the X, and where his sister had told him to find what belonged to him sat Reese. Was she waiting for him?

CHAPTER TWENTY-FIVE

She felt his presence before she saw him. It sounded silly, but her soul was connected to his in a way she couldn't explain. It was probably why Diana Ross and the Supremes demanded she "Stop in the Name of Love" on the way to Aspen Cove. It was also probably why Otis Redding reminded her why "These Arms of Mine" longed to hold him. It didn't stop her from wanting to drown some sense into the man, but she couldn't help herself from wanting him, caring for him, loving him. She hadn't known him for long, but her heart had known him forever.

"I thought you'd be in bed," he said as he walked up.

She scooted over and made room for him on the blanket.

"I tried, but emotions are a funny thing. First, there was anger at my mom, and then I felt sorry for her. I came out here to make sense of things."

"How's that going for you?"

"Oh, you know. I feel like a leaf in a cyclone."

She stared at him. "Are you going to sit or just throw shade on my moon tan?"

He took a seat beside her. "How is your mom?"

She looked toward the empty deck. "Probably drunk. If you're planning on sleeping in your room, you might get a surprise. I think she's in your bed."

He shook his head. "I didn't come back for my bed."

"Why did you come back?" She held up her hand. "Before you tell me. I need to say that you were right about so much. I don't know what we were thinking." She pointed between the two of them. "There's something between us but honestly, there's no—"

"Don't say it."

"Say what?"

"You were going to say there's no future for us, and you may be right. An hour ago, I would have agreed with you, but I've changed my mind."

She turned to face him. "What changed your mind?"

He pulled the pink envelope from his back pocket. "This led me here." He opened it and pointed to the writing. "X marks the spot." He pointed to her. "This spot." He took the white page his sister had written. "Find what belongs to you." He held it up. "Don't you see? I'd been taking care of her all my life, and this was her gift to me. She was leading me to you."

He dropped the pages onto the sand and pulled Reese into a kiss, and when he pulled away, he looked into her eyes. "I came for you. You can stay here with your mother, or you can come with me. I'm not going anywhere. If you stay, I'll be here in the morning knocking on your door with coffee and your favorite muffin."

"If I go with you?"

He smiled. "Baby, I'll bring you coffee and your favorite muffin in bed."

She hopped up. "Let me grab my things."

"What about your mom?"

She laughed as she ran toward the house. "She can get her own coffee and muffin."

She took the steps up the deck two at a time and found her mother sitting in the dark staring out the window at the lake.

"Are you leaving with him?"

"I am. Are you mad?" No matter what happened, she loved her mother. Love did funny things to people. It either lifted them up or weighted them down. She imagined her mother was once a dreamer who believed in happily ever afters. She fell in love with a boy who she had a summer fling with, and it didn't work out.

"No honey, I want you to be happy."

"I want you to be happy too, Mom. Have you thought about talking to my father now?"

Her mother smiled. "It's been so long sweetheart. Do you think it's wise?"

"Mom, he has a right to know, and I have a right to a father."

"Then you should tell him."

"Who is he?"

"If he's around, you can find him at the Big D Ranch."

"Oh, hell. If he's who I think he is, I bet he owns a shotgun."

Sara laughed. "If he's like his father, I'd say he owns several." She looked at Reese. "You should get your things. I'd like to ask your boyfriend a few questions."

Reese lifted her brows. Her mother was taking on that familiar motherly role. Her mother was more drill sergeant than anything else.

"Will you be nice?"

Her mother smiled. "Nice isn't what I'm known for, but I promise to be fair." She pointed to the chair across from her. "Have a seat young man."

Reese giggled. She normally wouldn't have left Brandon alone with her mother. It was like leaving a baby mouse in a nest of hungry eaglets, but he was a soldier and trained for combat. Curiosity nearly killed her, so she hid around the corner to listen and watch.

"What are your intentions toward my daughter?"

"Well, Ma'am. I don't rightly know where all this might lead. I'm not proposing marriage tonight because quite honestly neither of us are ready for that, but I'm not ruling it out in the future. I think your daughter is a remarkable woman. She's one of the smartest I know, which is a testament to you."

Reese wanted to swoon. She leaned in closer, so she didn't miss a word.

"Are you sucking up to me?"

"Yes, Ma'am, I am."

Her mother laughed. "I think I like you. Just remember that I am a veterinarian and I know how to put down big beasts. You treat my daughter right or you have to deal with me. I know she's told you stories and every one of them are true. In fact, she probably gave you the nice version because Reese is a romantic and tends to sugarcoat everything. I on the other hand won't pull any punches. My heart is honed from granite and when it bleeds it comes out thick and black like tar. I don't believe in love, but I want that for her now that I see what it means to her."

Most days she wanted to murder her mother, but she had a soft romantic side that Reese was seeing on this trip. There was hope for Sara Arden yet.

She rushed to her room and grabbed a few things then returned to the living room.

"I'm ready."

Brandon jumped to his feet and nodded to her mother.

"Thank you for your blessing."

Sara stood. "Son, you'd rather have that than my curse."

As they walked to the door her mother yelled. "Use a condom."

Reese waited until they weren't within earshot of the door.

"Are we sixteen?"

Brandon took the keys she offered and opened the door for her. "I kind of feel like it."

"Where are we headed?"

He smiled. "I got us a sweet place." He patted his leg "Let's go Z." The dog trotted after them to the car.

A few minutes later they were in the apartment above the bakery. Actually, they were in the bed in the apartment above the bakery and Brandon showed her just how much fun his gun could be.

The next morning she woke to the smell of muffins.

"Good morning love," the bed next to her sank and his lips brushed her cheek.

"Why are you up so early?"

"I made some promises." He held up a cup of coffee and a muffin. He pulled at the hem of his shirt and tugged it off. "You made me promise to make love to you again this morning after coffee and breakfast. You said you'd scream loud enough for the whole town to hear my name."

The heat rose to her cheeks. "I did not say that."

He shook his head. "No, but baby, I'd never silence you."

She had to give him credit. Not once did he silence her. In fact, during their lovemaking, he coaxed sounds from her that she wasn't sure she was capable of making.

"I may love you already," she said.

"You told me last night, and you can't take it back."

She wanted to crawl under the covers. There was no use denying what the heart already knew.

"I love you too. I think I knew it that moment when you stopped and were debating whether to let me in. I knew right then I wanted to wrap my fingers in your hair and kiss you."

"Show me."

He straddled her body and did exactly as she asked. The kiss lasted an hour and required the use of their last condom, but it was one helluva kiss.

"I picked up your computer because I knew you'd want to get back to Flame and Pertussis. Besides, I need to make sure he was a good lover."

"You feeling inadequate?" She rolled over and put her head on his chest. "Let me tell you about Flame. That man is hot, hot, hot. He was named correctly. He's got the sizzle in the sheets. Pertussis is ruined. There will never be another man for her."

"Good, she doesn't need another man. He's the only man she'll ever need."

"Brandon Fearless," she lifted on her elbow and looked him in the eye. "You're the only man I'll ever want or need."

"Don't forget that baby."

AN HOUR later they were in the diner eating one of Maisey's blue plate specials when the deputy sheriff and a pretty woman came inside.

"Aiden said to come by and get your uniforms when you're ready."

"Uniforms?" Reese asked.

Brandon smiled. "I hadn't gotten around to asking, but I thought maybe you and I could stick around a bit and make a go of it here in Aspen Cove. We can rent the apartment above the bakery and the sheriff offered me a job as a deputy."

Reese giggled. "Does it come with cuffs?" she teased. "I'm fairly sure there's a book about that somewhere."

The woman beside the deputy laughed. "It does." She thrust her hand forward. "I'm Poppy and this is Mark."

"Poppy? As in the flower?"

She nodded and sighed. "Yep, I'm the oldest bloom in the Dawson bouquet."

Realization dawned on Reese. She was staring into the eyes of her half-sister. She turned to Brandon. "I think staying in Aspen Cove is an excellent idea."

As soon as they were gone, Brandon looked at her. "You figured it out."

"My mom said that when she came back to tell my father about me, he already had more blooms started in another vase of flowers, so she didn't. She didn't want to disrupt his happiness and figured she'd already lived five years without his help."

The door opened and in walked Sara. She looked around the diner and her eyes stopped on them as if asking for permission to join them before she looked away.

"Do you mind if she joins us?"

Brandon shook his head. "Honey, your mother is a saint compared to mine."

Reese smiled. It was all perspective. There was always someone better and someone worse. In the scheme of things, she'd been lucky. Hers hadn't sold her for drugs.

"Mom, come and join us."

Sara smiled and hurried over. "Are you sure?"

"Absolutely," Brandon said. "I'd recommend the blue plate special."

"What is it?"

"It doesn't matter. It's always good."

Maisey walked over in her squeaky loafers with her swinging coffee pot. "Hey kids, what's it gonna be?"

Brandon held up three fingers. "Blue plates and coffees."

"And pie," Reese added.

"You'll get fat," her mother said.

Maisey smiled. "She's young. She'll burn it off." She winked. "How was the apartment?"

Sara rolled her eyes. "You might as well have mated in the center of Main Street. Doing anything in this town is like announcing it with a loudspeaker." She cupped her hand and stood. "Hello. In case you missed it. My daughter is having sex with the hot soldier named Brandon."

"Thanks, Mom, in case they missed it, now they are informed."

Her mother covered her face. "Oh. My. God. I can't believe I did that." She reached out and touched Reese's arm. "Honey, I'm so sorry. I don't know what's come over me. I'm not myself."

Reese laughed. "No, you're not, but I kind of like this person better. At least she's flawed and admits it. Mom, it's okay to be vulnerable. It's okay to not be okay. Sometimes you just need to let it all go. Maybe you should take a few weeks away from work and hang out at the beach house. I hear you're rich."

Her mom looked horrified.

"What the hell would I do there?"

"You don't have to do anything. Just be. I think that's part of your problem."

"I don't have a problem."

Brandon leaned back and watched the exchange. She could tell he was taking mental notes. He was a smart man and gathering intel.

"Your problem is that you don't see you have one. Just take a week to start. All you have to do is be here. That's all I'm asking."

"You want me here for a week?"

It wasn't that Reese wanted her here, but somewhere deep inside, she knew that her mother needed to be here. Healing happened in Aspen Cove and Sara Arden needed some.

The door to the diner opened and her mother stilled.

In fact, it seemed like the entire diner stilled though it was probably her imagination. In walked a tall cowboy wearing faded blue jeans and one of those white straw-like cowboy hats.

He looked around the diner and his eyes stopped on her mother, and Sara sucked in a breath.

"Sara? Is that you?"

He walked their way.

"Oh shit," her mother whispered. "Honey, I think I'll be staying that week."

THERE WERE three things Reese knew for sure when she arrived in Aspen Cove.

No one was interested in listening to her.

She couldn't rely on Z for all her emotional support.

Her damn muse was missing in action.

Since her arrival, her life had come full circle. Not only had her muse returned, but she brought Mr. Right with her, and he loved her dog as much as she did.

The novel she was struggling with might have the worst character names, but it was the best book she'd ever written.

While she'd closed the chapter on her past, she was opening the next book and penning the first chapter of her future, and seeing her mom look at Lloyd Dawson told her it was going to be a doozy.

CHECK out what happens when young love gets a second chance in One Hundred Chances.

OTHER BOOKS BY KELLY COLLINS

An Aspen Cove Romance Series

One Hundred Reasons

One Hundred Heartbeats

One Hundred Wishes

One Hundred Promises

One Hundred Excuses

One Hundred Christmas Kisses

One Hundred Lifetimes

One Hundred Ways

One Hundred Goodbyes

One Hundred Secrets

One Hundred Regrets

One Hundred Choices

One Hundred Decisions

One Hundred Glances

One Hundred Lessons

One Hundred Mistakes

One Hundred Nights

One Hundred Whispers

One Hundred Reflections

One Hundred Chances

JOIN MY READER'S CLUB AND GET A FREE BOOK.

Go to www.authorkellycollins.com

ABOUT THE AUTHOR

International bestselling author of more than thirty novels, Kelly Collins writes with the intention of keeping love alive. Always a romantic, she blends real-life events with her vivid imagination to create characters and stories that lovers of contemporary romance, new adult, and romantic suspense will return to again and again.

For More Information
www.authorkellycollins.com
kelly@authorkellycollins.com

CPSIA information can be obtained
at www.ICGtesting.com
Printed in the USA
BVHW050024140223
658395BV00025B/426